Rachel heard metal clank. Then she felt pricks on her arms and on the backs of her hands. Her vision kept blurring, and people moved like melting blobs of color. Plastic tubes snaked down from metal stands and were attached to her arms. She felt herself falling. The sounds faded. She was so tired. Blackness reached out to her. She welcomed it and swam into the black nothingness.

When Dreams SHATTER

by Lurlene McDaniel

Dedicated to my son, Sean,
twice a day, every day,
for the rest of his life.

Cover photo by John Strange

Published by Willowisp Press, Inc.
401 E. Wilson Bridge Road, Worthington, Ohio 43085

Based on *Will I Ever Dance Again?*

Printed in the United States of America

10 9 8 7 6 5 4 3 2

ISBN 0-87406-285-3

One

"**O**NE and two and stretch. And up, and down. Work with the inside of your leg, ladies. Yes, heel forward . . ." The thickly European-accented voice of Madame Tasha Pershoff hung over the rehearsal hall like a cloud.

Rachel Deering rose upward onto toe and stretched until she hurt before melting into a grand *plie*. All the while she kept her back perfectly aligned. Her body ached and every muscle felt tired. Her body hurt so bad that it was almost impossible for Rachel to concentrate on Madame Pershoff and her ballet class.

"Come, come, ladies!" Madame Pershoff scolded. "Straighten those backs. Hold those muscles."

Rachel's muscles begged for mercy as she performed with the rest of her advanced dance class. In the banks of mirrors in front of the barre, Rachel could see the reflection of Madame Pershoff. Madame Pershoff sat in her stiff-backed chair next to the piano, tapping time with her silver-headed cane on the dull oak floor of the studio. The tapping sounded like a sledgehammer in Rachel's ears.

She arched her arm above her head, then bent to touch her forehead to her knee. Oh, rats. I have to go to the bathroom again, she thought to herself. But she didn't dare ask to be excused. Madame Pershoff frowned on any type of interruption. Why were ballet dancers expected to have iron bladders anyway? Rachel wondered.

Rachel thought about how rotten the rest of her day had been. She had had a pop quiz in math and had been assigned over fifty pages of reading in history. Then, she had arrived late for ballet class. This was an unpardonable sin to Madame Pershoff of Miami's Corps de Ballet Dance Studio. Rachel's pointe shoes and legwarmers looked like they had been put on quickly and she looked a little sloppy in the full-length mirror.

"Rachel! Are you asleep today? Your barre work is poor." Madame Pershoff's sharp voice interrupted Rachel's thoughts.

"Sorry," Rachel muttered, feeling her face grow hot. Nothing was more embarrassing than being criticized in front of the entire class.

"First you are late. Then you throw on your exercise clothing. Now you seem half asleep during your exercises. This will not do, Rachel." Rachel felt humiliated. She had been a student of Madame's for eight years, ever since she was five. But she had never gotten used to being criticized in front of the whole class. At the moment, Rachel felt like chucking all her hopes for a career as a professional ballerina.

She gritted her teeth. "Forgive me," Rachel said contritely, watching Madame Pershoff's hands gripping the ornate head of the shiny ebony cane. Sometimes Rachel hated the woman. Sometimes she loved her. But she always respected her. Madame Pershoff did not waste her time on students whom she didn't think had talent. If Rachel was ever to become a professional dancer, then Madame Pershoff was the only one to help her.

"Is there some reason for this lapse of yours?"

"I don't feel very well today," Rachel said softly.

"Then perhaps you should sit down."

"I'll be fine." Rachel wished she could disappear as she felt the eyes of every other member of the class focus on her.

"Very well." Madame Pershoff nodded to the pianist, who began playing as if no interruption had occurred. Rachel knew that many dance studios had recorded music, but not Madame Pershoff's. Only live music would suit the once-great European dancer. Her accented voice counted, "One and two and up and down . . ."

Rachel struggled for a few more moments before finally admitting to herself that it was no use. She had to go to the bathroom. She caught Madame Pershoff's eye and slipped away from the barre. Quietly, she stole into the dressing area of the studio.

Jeans, blouses, shoes, and books were piled on the floor and benches. They had been abandoned by girls who had hurried in from the hot September afternoon to change into leotards, tights, and pointe shoes. For two hours every day, as long as Rachel could remember, she'd practiced ballet. Except on Saturdays when she practiced for four hours. When there was a dance concert planned, the classes were even longer and even more demanding.

But the live performances that showcased Madame Pershoff's top students were all Rachel lived for. She loved to walk out onstage and see the lights. She loved to hear the strains of classical music and the applause after a performance. To dance—that's what Rachel Deering worked so hard for, those glorious moments onstage when she became one with the music.

Rachel left the bathroom and darted back to the barre. Darn! She'd forgotten to get a drink of water. She was thirsty a lot lately. In fact, ever since she'd had the flu, two weeks before, Rachel had felt lousy. She'd felt tired, thirsty, and worn out.

Madame Pershoff halted the warm-up work. "We will begin working in pairs, but first I will announce my plans for the Christmas holidays."

Instantly, Rachel forgot all her physical complaints and focused her attention on Madame Pershoff. "This year's concert will be downtown at the old Olympus Theater. We will be performing *Swan Lake*." A buzz of whispers started through the class. *Swan Lake!* It was every dancer's dream to dance the *pas de deux* and the solo of the Dying Swan.

Madame Pershoff had only four students capable of competing for the coveted role. Rachel ticked them off mentally. They were herself, Pat Cummings, Jill Menes and . . . Automatically, her eyes looked into the mirror.

There she saw the challenging eyes of her main competition, Melanie Hallick, look coolly back at her. For a moment the two girls surveyed one another in the glass.

Rachel was tall and slim with chestnut hair, brown eyes, and the unmistakable carriage of a dancer, even to the slightly outward turned feet that gave her a ducklike walk. Melanie was not nearly so tall, and she had pale blond hair, and ice-blue eyes. Rachel had often envied how petite Melanie was. She sometimes felt like a horse next to her. Her height looked good on the dance floor, but it made her feel self-conscious to be the tallest eighth grader at Miami Junior High School.

". . . choose one for the part," Madame Pershoff was saying. "And as a special favor to me, an old friend, a dance instructor in New York, will be attending while he's visiting Miami for the holidays."

The news sent a tingling sensation up Rachel's spine. The concert was only three months away. She'd have to work extra hard if she was going to compete for the solo. Jill and Pat were no real competition, but Melanie was a different story. All Rachel's dance life, the two of them had competed for the top parts. Whatever Rachel wanted, Melanie seemed to want, too.

She shot Melanie a final look in the mirror and stooped to adjust her pointe shoe. It wouldn't be so bad if Melanie was at least a pleasant human being. But she wasn't. She was cool and aloof. Rachel had given up trying to befriend her years before.

"Well, this is one thing you won't get, Melanie," Rachel said under her breath. "This part is going to be mine." Rachel swallowed determinedly and realized her throat was so dry it burned. And she had to go to the bathroom, again.

* * * * *

"Sorry, I'm late, dear. But I had to take Chris for new ballet slippers. How was class?"

Rachel scooted across the seat in her mother's car and flopped in exhaustion against the seat. Chris, her nine-year-old sister, was a real pain. "It was all right. But I'm pooped."

Her mother maneuvered the car into the traffic. "You look tired. You have dark circles under your eyes. You should try to get more rest dear."

Swell. I look like a raccoon. What a stinking day, Rachel thought. Then she said, "It just takes a while to adjust to the school schedule after summer vacation. Besides, it's so hot."

She lifted her long hair off her neck and turned to let the air conditioning blow on her bare skin. She'd thought about cutting her hair a hundred times, but Madame Pershoff liked long hair on her dancers, especially slicked back in a bun and adorned with fancy headpieces.

They continued home while Rachel's mother chattered about her day. Rachel only half-listened as they rolled along. When they pulled into their palm tree lined driveway, Rachel bolted from the car and through the front door to her bedroom. Pink carpeting set off her white wicker furniture.

Rachel fell across her bed, glad to be alone in her room. She reached over to flip on her tape deck, only to discover that her prized tape of *Swan Lake* was missing. She sat up. Darn that Chris! Rachel hurried into the kitchen and found Chris helping her mother make a salad. "Mom! Chris went into my room again. And without my permission."

Chris looked at Mrs. Deering innocently. "I did not."

"She stole my tape. I want a lock for my door."

"I bought it for your birthday last February. I like to listen to it, too."

Rachel glared at her kid sister. The skinny

little brat! Chris had been taking ballet for two years from Madame Pershoff, but she still hadn't developed much grace. Chris was such a copycat. She'd never have thought to take ballet lessons if Rachel wasn't taking them. "Well, give it back this minute!"

"Now girls, stop it," Rachel's mother said.

"But, Mom . . ."

"Rachel! That's enough. Chris," Mrs. Deering warned, "you know you're not supposed to go into Rachel's room without permission. Now go get her tape."

Chris frowned at Rachel and stomped out of the kitchen. A few minutes later she returned with the missing tape.

Rachel retreated to her room and put the tape into her deck. She closed her eyes and saw herself in a white satin tutu, floating across the stage. She was so tired and thirsty. But she wanted that part. More than anything, she wanted that part.

Two

"RACHEL, for goodness sake, take it easy. That's the third glass of orange juice you've gulped down this morning." The words came from Rachel's father, who was studying the newspaper between bites of breakfast.

"Sorry." Rachel set the juice glass down guiltily. "I don't know why I'm so thirsty this morning. Maybe it's because I dreamed I was crawling through the desert all night."

Mr. Deering smiled at his daughter. Rachel thought her father was very distinguished with his dark hair and hazel eyes. "Are you feeling all right? You look tired," he asked.

Rachel smiled back at him brightly. "I'm feeling great. And with the recital coming up, I'd like to take extra night classes at the studio."

"Oh, honey, I hate to see you work so hard,"

Mrs. Deering said as she came alongside the table.

"Mom, please. You know how much these parts mean to me. I can't expect to get them if I don't work for them." Or beat out Melanie for the roles, she added mentally.

"Where's Chris? I said I'd drop her off at her school today, but she's running late," her father interrupted.

"I have no idea," Rachel answered her father, grateful to change the subject.

Chris rushed into the large, sunny kitchen and scooted into her seat. "I'm late because Rachel hogged the bathroom," she complained.

"I did not."

"You did too. What do you do in there anyway?"

"Now, girls," Mrs. Deering interrupted. "Let's not argue. Chris, hurry up and eat. You're father has to leave. Rachel . . ."

"I'm on my way," Rachel called. She scooped up her books from the counter and headed out the door before her mother could begin a lecture. She hurried along, forcing a bouncy rhythm into her step that she did not feel. A block from her home, she slowed down and wiped perspiration off her brow. It was going to be a long hot day and she was already exhausted before she arrived at the corner.

* * * * *

The noise of the cafeteria and the smell of greasy food made Rachel feel sick to her stomach as she sat down at the cafeteria table during lunch time. "Hi," she said to Jenny Brady, her best friend.

"Hi yourself. If you like living dangerously, eat the spaghetti. Otherwise, stick to the pudding." Jenny's perky greeting made Rachel feel better. Jenny was the class clown and it was always fun to be around her. Sometimes, Rachel wondered why they'd been such good friends through elementary school and now junior high. They didn't have much in common. Jenny didn't dance a step, and dance was Rachel's whole life. Jenny was outgoing and talkative. Rachel was shy and quiet.

"Thanks for the inside information." Rachel pushed aside her tray. "I don't feel much like eating anyway. I'm just going to drink my milk. Do you want yours?"

"Are you kidding? Milk is too close to health food for me. Give me cola anytime. So how's it going in the world of ballet?"

Rachel smiled. "I guess it'll go fine if I can find the energy to take two classes a day from now until Madame Pershoff decides to hold the competition for the Christmas concert."

16

"You really want it that bad? You look sort of burned out to me."

"Thanks a lot!" Rachel poked Jenny playfully on the arm. "According to Madame Pershoff, an important friend of hers will be here to watch. I don't want to miss the chance to impress some mysterious stranger." Rachel let her eyes roam the cafeteria. Her vision stopped cold on Nick Carter, who had just come in with a few of his friends. Rachel's pulse raced and she turned her attention quickly back to Jenny.

"Did Nick come in?" Jenny asked.

Rachel sucked up a mouthful of milk and pretended she didn't notice. "Oh, I guess he did. Who cares?"

"From the looks of it, you do."

"Nick Carter doesn't know I'm alive. And besides, what would it matter if he did? I haven't got time for boys."

Jenny shrugged and then smiled toward the doorway. "Ah . . . there's Ben." Jenny waved to a broad-shouldered boy with sandy-blond curly hair.

Rachel tried not to be jealous. Ben Coleman and Jenny had been an item since the first day of school. And now that Jenny had an honest-to-goodness boyfriend, Rachel was afraid that their friendship would have to take a backseat. In some ways Rachel was happy for Jenny. In others, it bothered her. She felt left out. Lately, she had begun wondering what it would be like to have a boyfriend of her own. But how could she? All of her spare time was spent dancing. "Look," Rachel said, rising from the table. "I'll leave you two alone since I need to stop off at the bathroom before class." At least that much was true.

"Call me tonight," Jenny said as she left.

"After my dance class. Sure thing." Rachel picked up her tray and headed to the dirty tray window where she almost collided with Nick Carter. "Excuse me," she mumbled. She looked into Nick's deep brown eyes.

Nick's hand reached out to steady her tray. "No problem."

Then he stepped to one side. She stepped to the same side. He stepped the other way— and she stepped with him in perfect unity. "Stand still," he directed with a hint of laughter in his voice.

"Uh-sorry . . ." she managed to say over her embarrassment.

"You go this way and I'll go that way," Nick said, pointing in opposite directions. She swallowed hard and nodded and finally the two of them got past each other.

She held her breath as he made his way to a

far table where he sat down across from Melanie Hallick. That figures, Rachel thought. Melanie will go after him, too.

Rachel squared her shoulders and watched Melanie lean over and whisper to Nick. They both looked in Rachel's direction. They were talking about her! Rachel was sure they were. She looked away from them and as she did she felt her tray tilt. Her plate fell to the floor with a crash.

The noise echoed through the cafeteria and all the chatter stopped. Every eye in the room turned to her direction. Rachel wished she could melt and tears filled her eyes. She mumbled an apology to the woman behind the window. Then she ran from the cafeteria to the safety of the girl's room where she splashed cold water on her burning face. Quickly, she applied fresh makeup. All the while, she thought about the smirk on Melanie's face.

Rachel sighed. At least she knew the score. Melanie had Nick. Jenny had Ben. But Rachel Deering was going to get the part of the prima ballerina for the Christmas dance concert. She didn't need or want anything else.

* * * * *

"I'm telling you, it's impossible!" Jenny

wailed in Rachel's ear through the phone receiver. "I'm too young to spend the rest of my life chained to a history book. Who cares what the Romans did? They're all dead now."

Rachel tried to listen to Jenny, but she was exhausted. After a full day of school and two dance classes, she was ready to drop. "Uh . . . Jen, I have to go. Chris is begging for the phone."

"No problem. Ben's supposed to call me anyway."

Rachel hung up and went to the bathroom. In the mirror, her face looked pink, almost as if she'd been out in the sun. She stuck out her tongue and stared at it in the mirror.

"Are you in there again?" Chris' voice came through the open doorway.

"Get lost," Rachel said.

"Every time I walk by, you're in there," Chris grumbled, flouncing her long brown hair.

"So what? Do you have the toilet paper concession?"

"Mom," Chris shouted. "Rachel's talking mean to me again."

Mrs. Deering came in from her bedroom. "Now what?"

But Rachel was too tired to argue. "Never mind," she said. "I'm going to bed early tonight."

"Rachel, are you all right?" Mrs. Deering looked at her through narrowed eyes.

"Good grief, yes. Can't I just go to bed early if I want?"

Her mother took her by the shoulders and led her down the hallway. "Let's go to your room. I want to talk to you."

Rachel obeyed, stretching out on her bed and bracing herself for her mother's lecture. "I'm sorry I fussed at Chris."

"That will never change," Mrs. Deering said. "It's not your and Chris' relationship I want to discuss. It's you. Honey, your dad and I are concerned about you."

"Why?"

"You seem so tired lately. And with your thirst and bathroom routine—"

"Oh, Mom, honestly. I've just never completely gotten over the flu from a few weeks back."

"Well if it is the flu, I want it checked out."

"Like how?" Rachel quizzed her mother nervously.

"Go by Dr. Stein's office tomorrow before ballet class—"

"Dr. Stein!" Rachel sat upright on the bed. "The *baby* doctor."

"He's a pediatrician, Rachel. And he's *your* pediatrician, I might add. Dr. Stein is a good doctor. You've seen him for years."

"But that's only when I need shots or something. I don't want to go to a baby doctor. Not when I'm perfectly fine."

Mrs. Deering placed her hands on her hips. "There will be no arguing about this, Rachel. I've already made the appointment. I'll pick you up early from school and drop you off. Then I'll go get Chris for her dentist appointment. If you finish before I get back, just catch the city bus to dance class. You've taken the bus plenty of times before."

"You know how Madame Pershoff gets if you're late to her class . . ."

"You won't be late. All Dr. Stein wants to do is a few quick tests right there in his office."

The tone of her mother's voice convinced Rachel that there was no discussing the matter. She'd have to go see Dr. Stein. Rachel crawled between the sheets of her bed still mad at her parents. Why did they treat her like such a kid? After all, Madame Pershoff considered her a top ballet student. She was good enough to perform in important concerts. Well, one day, she'd be grown and would have her own apartment and would take dance classes all day long. There would be no one to tell her what to do. No one to run her life except herself.

Three

"YOU smell funny," Chris said, wrinkling her nose in Rachel's direction at the breakfast table the next morning.

"Thanks a lot." Even after a long night's sleep, Rachel felt tired. "Maybe it's my perfume."

"No. It's not like perfume." Chris screwed up her face in thought. Then she snapped her fingers. "I know! Fingernail polish. That's what you smell like. Did you paint your nails? I'll bet you did!"

Rachel dangled unpainted nails under her sister's nose. "See, smarty. No polish. Honestly, Chris, I think something's wrong with your nose."

"There is not."

"There is too."

"Girls," Mrs. Deering interrupted. "Rachel, why aren't you eating?"

"I'm not hungry," she said. The truth was that she felt sick to her stomach. But she didn't want her mother to know or she might keep her home from school and dance classes. "I've got to run anyway." Rachel gulped down her orange juice, but it did little to soothe her thirst.

"Just a minute," Mrs. Deering called before Rachel could bolt out the door. "Don't forget, I'm picking you up at two-thirty and dropping you at Dr. Stein's."

"I won't forget." Rachel hurried out the door and started toward the school bus stop. Her feet dragged behind her like lead weights. I'm going to have to feel a whole lot better really soon if I'm going to compete for that part, she told herself. She'd seen Melanie the night before. Melanie was taking an extra class, too, so Rachel knew that Melanie was working hard to get the part. But Rachel knew that Madame Pershoff would choose whomever danced the best for the solo. She would show no favorites. Sometimes she'd chosen Melanie, sometimes she'd chosen Rachel for top honors.

In spite of all her protests to her mother, Rachel was relieved to be going to the doctor. She really hadn't been feeling like herself lately. This morning when she'd put on her blouse, she'd noticed that her ribs were showing through her skin. That meant she was losing weight. Rachel wanted to look like a dying swan not a dead one! Rachel smiled at her own dark humor.

The school day crawled by. Rachel stopped at every drinking fountain in the halls before and after classes. By lunchtime she was convinced that she wasn't going to make it through the day. "Just a few more hours," she told herself. After the doctor checked her and maybe gave her some medicine, she could get on with her life.

Rachel climbed the stairs to the second floor for math class. She was late, and the tardy bell had already rung. But, she didn't care. She felt so weak. Then she felt dizzy and sick to her stomach. Rachel dropped her books and clung to the railing. She staggered, then felt strong hands grab her.

"Are you all right?"

Rachel turned and looked into the brown eyes of Nick Carter. He held her arm and steadied her against the wall. "No," she said, feeling hot and then clammy cold. She felt too woozy to even be self-conscious in his presence.

"Here. Sit down on the stairs for a minute." She obeyed without saying a word. He sat next to her, all the while holding her arm. "If you feel faint, put your head between your knees. My football coach taught me that when I got hurt on the field."

Rachel ducked her head. "Breathe deep," Nick said.

She took long gulps of air. Finally, her head cleared and she felt like she was back in control of her body. She raised her head slowly. "Th-thanks. That helped."

His firm grip on her arm loosened and he slipped his arm around her waist. "Do you think you can stand?"

"Maybe."

"I'll help you to the clinic."

"Oh, I don't want to go there . . ." She tried to protest, but he was helping her to stand and her legs still felt wobbly. She was forced to lean against him. His side felt secure and warm.

"I don't think you have a choice," he told her, guiding her down the stairs toward the clinic.

"My books . . ."

"I'll pick them up and bring them to the clinic for you."

She was too weak to protest so she let him lead her. At the clinic, the nurse took over and offered to call Rachel's mother.

"No, that's okay. She's coming to pick me up in an hour anyway. Maybe if I lie here a while . . ."

The nurse agreed and Rachel stretched out on the starched white bed. The air conditioning hummed and cooled her. She relaxed while her strength slowly returned. Then Rachel remembered that she'd never even thanked Nick. She thought about telling Jenny that Nick put his arm around her. Then she figured it wouldn't mean much to her friend. After all, Ben put his arm around Jenny all the time. Drained and exhausted, Rachel drifted into a light sleep and dreamed of Nick Carter.

By two-thirty, she felt better. She collected her books—Nick had brought them by—and went to meet her mother. "How was your day?" Mrs. Deering asked.

Guiltily, Rachel said, "Fine." She knew that if she told about her dizzy spell, her mother would demand that she skip dance class. And that was something Rachel didn't want to do. She was feeling better. The nap in the clinic had helped her a lot.

In the parking lot, her mother reminded, "If I miss you, catch the bus. I'll pick you up at the studio."

Rachel waved good-bye and put her dance bag over her shoulder. She entered the doctor's office. Rachel was glad to be inside and away from the heat. But everywhere she looked she saw babies and young children. Most of them were fussing. The noise made her head throb. She approached the nurse's window and rang the bell.

"Rachel, hello," Miss Wimberly greeted through the glass partition. "Booming business today. I think every child in Coral Gables is sick. We're running behind, but the doctor definitely wants to see you. If you'll just wait in the outer room—"

"Wait?" Rachel interrupted. "But I have dance class. I can't be late."

"It won't be that long. We'll need to do a finger prick, but Dr. Stein wants to discuss your symptoms with you." *A finger prick.* Ugh! Rachel hated needles, even tiny ones that only poked her fingertip. Just then, Miss Wimberly's phone rang. "Go sit down, Rachel, and I'll be with you as soon as possible."

The nurse shut the partition and Rachel shuffled across the room. She sat down between a crying infant and a cranky toddler. After twenty minutes, she still had not been called. She began to fidget, glancing nervously at her wristwatch. The moments dragged by, and her stomach began to tighten. If the doctor was any later, she would miss her bus and be late for her dance class.

Rachel drummed her fingers on the arm of the chair. The bus was due in five minutes. If she left right now, she'd just make it. Sure, her mother would be angry that she didn't keep the appointment, but she'd tried hadn't she? It wasn't her fault that the doctor was running so far behind schedule. Maybe tomorrow his office would be less crowded.

Rachel made up her mind not to wait any longer. She stood, shook off a spell of lightheadedness, and picked up her dance bag. She stopped for a drink at the fountain in the waiting room, but the water didn't satisfy her burning thirst.

Rachel slipped out into the bright, hot sunlight and started for the bus bench, unaware that Miss Wimberly had just called her name inside the office.

* * * * *

"You don't look sick to me," Melanie said.

Rachel stopped struggling with her tights and stared up at Melanie. "I'm fine now," Rachel lied, knowing she'd just applied makeup to conceal the deep, dark circles under her eyes.

"Nick told me he had to practically carry

you to the clinic. But I see you're not too sick for dance class."

Rachel gritted her teeth and fought back her pounding headache. Melanie's accusatory tone just made it worse. Melanie probably thought she'd been faking it. She probably thought Rachel had thrown herself at Nick in the hall. "I really felt faint at the time, Melanie. Nick happened to be passing by and he helped me out. I certainly didn't mean to upset you."

"Who's upset? I was making an observation, that's all." Melanie stomped out of the dressing area into the studio.

Rachel continued to dress, more determined to beat out Melanie than ever. She'd show Melanie Hallick a thing or two! She slipped on her ballet slippers for barre work and joined her fellow dancers at the barre in front of the mirrors. *Good grief, I look thin . . .* She ignored her reflection and concentrated. *Releve . . . plie . . . again. Stretch . . . bend . . . again.*

Rachel lifted her leg and stretched far to the side. Then she felt a wave of dizziness sweep over her. Rachel gripped the barre and waited for her head to clear. Don't let me faint here in class, she pleaded silently. She attempted the maneuver a second time, more slowly this time.

Why is the floor tilting? she wondered. The

world began to spin around her in slow motion. Why am I falling? Why is everyone shouting at me? The floor rose and met her. Voices called her name but she couldn't answer. She fought against the blackness that was engulfing her.

Sirens, she heard sirens. Then she heard men's voices and felt strong hands lifting her. Someone was crying. Who? Probably Pat. She cried over everything. Don't cry for me, she tried to say.

Fingers forced open her eyes. A bright beam of light was shown into them. Rachel struggled to keep them shut. A man said, "She's almost comatose." What's that? Rachel wondered.

She felt herself being lifted and laid on a bed with wheels. She wanted to get up, but she couldn't. She felt the bed roll and then she was lifted into a car . . . no . . . a truck? An ambulance? "Why?" she whispered.

"Hang in there, little lady," a voice said.

The next thing Rachel knew she was being pushed down a corridor. Lights zoomed by overhead. Then she was in a large room. There were more faces. There were men and women in white coats. Were they doctors? Nurses? "I want my mother . . ."

"She's on her way, honey . . ."

Then there were more voices, barking

orders and commands. "Blood pressure."

"What's her temp . . ."

"Pulse?"

"She's dehydrated. We'll need some IVs, saline. *Stat!*"

"Smell that acetone. She's swimming in acetone."

Then Rachel felt her mother beside her, stroking her forehead. "Rachel, baby . . . honey, it's me. I'm here, honey."

"Mom . . . I'm cold." She smelled alcohol, biting and sharp. A man's deep voice demanded, "Get her to ICU and on monitors."

Rachel heard metal clank. Then she felt pricks on her arms and on the backs of her hands. Her vision kept blurring, and people moved like melting blobs of color. Plastic tubes snaked down from metal stands and were attached to her arms. She felt herself falling. The sounds faded. The voices echoed dimly. She was so tired. Blackness reached out to her. She welcomed it and swam into the black nothingness.

Four

"WELCOME back to the real world, Rachel Deering." Those were the first words Rachel heard when she opened her eyes. The words came from a man dressed in a white lab coat with light brown hair. He had a neatly trimmed beard. He held out his hand. "I'm Dr. Malar. You're in the hospital and you've been a pretty sick girl, but you're going to be fine." His kind blue eyes and broad smile reinforced his words.

"Where are my parents?" Her voice was weak and raspy.

"Just outside. I'll get them."

When her parents entered, Rachel noticed that they both looked worried. After they both hugged her, she asked, "What happened to me?"

Her parents looked at each other. Dr. Malar cleared his throat and gave her a comforting look. "The technical term is *ketoacidosis*. It's the last stage of the disease, diabetes mellitus."

Rachel gasped. "I have diabetes? That can't be true." Rachel wasn't even sure what diabetes was, only that it had something to do with sugar and shots. "Am I—will I die?"

"Goodness, no," Dr. Malar said with a reassuring pat. "But you've got a lot to learn over the next few days."

Then the memory of her collapse in dance class came back to her. "How long have I been asleep?"

"Two days," Dr. Malar said.

She looked up at him in shock. "Two days? That's impossible."

"Diabetic acidosis is very serious, Rachel. We've got you stabilized now, but you were very sick." He picked up the IV tube attached to her arm. "How'd you like some real food instead of this liquid stuff? I'll have a nurse remove it and start you on the real thing this evening."

"I'm not very hungry," she confessed.

"You will be," he assured her. "Now that we've got your blood chemistry in order, you'll start feeling normal again."

"I was feeling pretty crummy."

"We know," her mother said. "If you hadn't

left Dr. Stein's office, he would have discovered the diabetes from the blood test."

"Sorry," she muttered. "But it was getting so late." She caught the doctor's eye again. "When can I go home?"

"In a few days."

"But I have school. And dance class." Rachel felt panicked. She couldn't miss even a few days. She needed every minute of practice to get in shape for the audition.

"Don't worry. You'll be able to dance again. But first you've got to learn how to take care of yourself. I'm a pediatric endocrinologist. That's a fancy way to say a specialist in juvenile diabetes. I'll be your doctor, and you've got plenty to learn over the next few days. I'll be teaching you about insulin and insulin reactions. My nurse, Anne, will help you learn to monitor and manage your disease. And a dietician will help you learn a proper diet. You'll even get to meet some other kids your age with diabetes."

Rachel blinked up at him. She didn't want to meet other kids. She didn't want to learn about diabetes. She just wanted to go home. Dr. Malar patted her shoulder. "We'll let you get some rest now. I'll be back later and begin with some of the basics."

After they left, Rachel stared straight up at

the ceiling. Why was this happening to her? Two weeks before she'd been normal. She had dreamed of dancing in a ballet company. Now, she had a serious disease. She was a freak. Now she needed special diets and managing and—what? Tears slid from the corners of her eyes. What else did she need they hadn't told her about?

* * * * *

Dr. Malar returned later that evening along with his assistant, Anne. Anne was a pretty woman with jet black hair that turned under on the ends and brushed her shoulders every time she moved her head.

"Hi," Anne said, cheerfully. "How'd dinner taste?"

"Not as bad as it looked," Rachel said. "I guess I was hungrier than I thought. But I've lost weight, haven't I?"

"It's a part of your illness," Dr. Malar explained. Ketoacidosis is a little complicated, Rachel. I'm going to try to explain what happened to you."

She scooted up on her pillow and hunched her knees beneath the covers. Her hospital ID bracelet dangled on her thin wrist.

"When you have diabetes, your pancreas

36

stops making insulin. And without insulin, the food you eat can't be used by your cells. Think of insulin as a house key. It opens the doors of your cells. Do you know what cells are?"

"The little tiny parts that make up my body," Rachel said, remembering her basic biology.

"That's right. And without the key of insulin, *glucose*—that's another name for sugar—can't get inside your cells to be used for food. So, all of the food you were eating was turned into glucose. But then the glucose couldn't get into the cells to provide energy for your body. In a way, you were eating, but starving to death."

Her eyes grew wide. "Really? Where did the glucose go?"

"It built up and floated in your blood stream. You were thirsty all the time, weren't you?"

"Yes. I couldn't get enough to drink."

"And you went to the bathroom a lot?"

"I figured the one caused the other," she said with a shrug.

Dr. Malar laughed. "Those symptoms were simply your body's way of trying to flush out all the free-floating glucose. In desperation for food, your body started breaking down fat and protein for energy. This made you build up acetone. You even smelled like the stuff."

"Like fingernail polish remover?" Rachel asked, remembering Chris' words from some days before at the breakfast table.

Anne smiled. "It smells a little like that."

"But, of course, people are meant to run on glucose. Your body couldn't flush it all out. The job was too great. Your system went into overload or, in medical terms, ketoacidosis. But all that's behind you now. With insulin, proper diet and exercise, you can live with diabetes. It's important that you learn how."

Already Rachel's mind was swimming with information. And now they were telling her she had more to learn. Yet, they'd also said she couldn't leave until she learned it all. She sighed, trying not to feel so overwhelmed. All she wanted was to get out of the hospital—and soon! "So when do I start learning?"

Anne said, "Right now." She reached into her lab coat and pulled out a syringe and a small vial filled with a milky liquid. "This is an insulin syringe and a bottle of insulin. Now that you're off the IVs, you'll have to learn to administer your own dose of insulin, so I'm going to show you how to draw it up and how to give yourself the shots—"

"Now wait a minute," Rachel interrupted, her attention glued to the sharp, shiny needle on the end of the syringe. "I can't give myself a shot."

"All juvenile diabetics do," Dr. Malar said, crossing his arms over his chest. "And there are millions in the world."

"Well, count me out."

Dr. Malar took her hand. "Rachel, there's no other way to get the insulin inside your body. It's a short needle and only goes right under your skin."

To Rachel, the needle looked a foot long. "Don't you have any pills?"

"Pills won't work on juvenile diabetes. Researchers are testing a pill that might stand up to the acids in a person's stomach, but for right now, shots are the only way."

She swallowed hard, knowing that if she didn't cooperate, she'd never get out of the hospital. "Well . . . okay. I guess I can do anything for a few days."

Anne and Dr. Malar eyed one another. "You'll have to administer insulin twice a day, Rachel," Anne told her.

Her heart plummeted. "For how long?" She asked. "How long will I have to take the shots? A few weeks? A month?"

"Forever, Rachel. For the rest of your life."

"And if I don't?"

"Then you will die. It's as serious as that."

Five

RACHEL Deering cried long after Dr. Malar and Anne left. She lay in the hospital bed and cried until her pillow was soaked and her eyes were red and swollen. She made her way into the private bathroom adjoining her room and stared at herself in the mirror. Awful. I look awful. She thought. But what did it matter? She felt as if her entire life were over. She would be forever chained to needles and insulin and an illness.

When her parents came that night, she still felt awful. "Did you know I have to take shots two times a day?" she asked them.

"Yes," her mother said.

"Well, I think it stinks," Rachel answered.

"So do we," her father said. "I'd take your place in a minute."

"Well, you can't," she snapped. "No one can do it for me." She picked at her bedcovers.

"It's not fair. Why did this happen to me? How did I get diabetes anyway?"

"I've been doing a lot of reading," Mrs. Deering said, brushing her hand through Rachel's hair. "Everything I could get my hands on, in fact. It seems that diabetes is hereditary."

"Who has it? Why didn't I know about it?" Rachel asked angrily.

"My grandmother. But she didn't get it until she was eighty. And we think an aunt of your father's had it. There's a virus involved with it too."

"You mean I caught it? Like the flu?"

"Sort of. But you can't catch it if you don't have the genes for it. It's a combination of things."

"Well, I hate it."

Mr. Deering let out a deep breath. "You can choose many things in life, Rachel. But you can't choose your ancestors. We're carriers of the diabetic genes. All of us."

"Can this happen to Chris?" For the first time she thought of her sister. Chris might be a brat but Rachel didn't want Chris to have to go through what she was going through.

"It could, but they can do a blood test that will predict if that's likely to happen."

Rachel couldn't decide what was worse,

having it happen unexpectedly, or knowing it was going to happen. "Can they make it go away? Don't they do research or something? I've seen telethons on TV . . ."

"They do plenty of research, but for right now, there are no cures." Hopeless. Rachel felt hopeless and suddenly angry.

Her mother said, "Dr. Malar told us that diabetics lead good, healthy lives. As long as you take care of yourself, you can do all the things you did before."

"I don't care," Rachel bristled. "I'm never going to get well. I'm never going to be normal again. I have diabetes and it's all your fault."

* * * * *

"You can do it, Rachel. Prepare the site like I showed you," Anne urged.

Rachel sat on the side of her hospital bed the next morning, the insulin syringe cradled in her palm. She'd filled it like Anne had shown her, thumping out the air bubbles and checking for accuracy of the dose. She handled it as if it were a snake. "I—I don't think I can do it," she confessed, fear running through her.

"The first one's the hardest."

Sunlight streamed in through the window,

filling the room with rich yellow light. Rachel longed to be outdoors. It was Saturday. Normally she'd be on her way to the studio for dance class by now. She asked, "Will it hurt?"

"A little. Insulin stings going in. Don't tense up. Relax your leg muscle. Pinch up the skin and inject the syringe."

With trembling fingers, Rachel wiped the cool alcohol swab over her leg three times, trying to work up her courage. She held the syringe over the site and watched the tip of the needle shake in her grip. Suddenly, she jabbed downward and felt the needle slide into her leg. Quickly, she pushed the plunger, pulled out the needle and smoothed the swab back over the site. It *had* stung, but she was pleased with herself. She'd done it!

"Good for you, Rachel," Anne praised.

Dr. Malar walked into the room. "So how'd it go?"

"I did it," Rachel said. "But it hurt—a *lot*."

"I know it did."

"Sure! How would you know?" She didn't understand why she felt so angry at him.

"Because I've been there." He reached inside his shirt collar and pulled out a round metal disk on a chain. "This is a Medic Alert medallion." He held it up for her to see a bright red insignia. "Anyone who has a health problem should wear one at all times. Your mother's already ordered yours." He turned it over where she read: *John L. Malar, Diabetes.*

"So you see, Rachel, I know very well what you're going through."

* * * * *

"How To Eat Like a King on a Diabetic Diet, Your Exchange Diet Plan." Rachel read the titles aloud from brochures that the hospital dietician had left with her. She leafed through one and read, "Six saltines equal one bread exchange. One half cup of yogurt equals one milk exchange . . ." She flipped through another. "Always carry candy in the event of an insulin reaction . . . ." What's that? she wondered. She didn't know if she could take any more information forced on her. Tears welled up in her eyes, and she hurled the pamphlets across the room.

A nightmare. That's what her life had turned into—a living nightmare. It was simply too much for one person to cope with or think about. There would be no more french fries and milkshakes, no more ice cream pig-outs. She recalled concoctions she and Chris had invented—ice cream mounds slathered with hot fudge, whipped cream, sugar sprinkles, and chocolate chips. Just thinking about it made her stomach growl. It was like saying good-bye to an old friend. From now on Rachel would have to consider every morsel she put in her mouth. It wasn't fair. It just wasn't fair!

Mrs. Deering found her curled into a tight ball on her bed. "Honey, what's wrong?"

Rachel turned her back on her mother. "I've got diabetes. I may as well be dead."

"Don't say that, Rachel. Don't even think it."

"Well, it's true. I'll never be able to do anything again—*ever*!"

"That's not true," Mrs. Deering said, smoothing Rachel's hair with her hand. Rachel jerked away. "You know, all your friends have been calling. Jenny, Francine, Marcie. Jenny wants to come by for a visit."

"No way," Rachel snapped. "I don't want to see anybody. I don't want people knowing about my shots and my special diet. No one!" she added for emphasis. "I'm a freak."

"No, you aren't," Mrs. Deering said, taking her by the shoulders. "Your friends care about you and they still want to be your friends. You can't change what's happened, but you can change your attitude about it."

Rachel offered her mother a deep, dark

scowl. Mrs. Deering added, "Madame Pershoff wants to come by, too."

"Please, no. Not Madame," Rachel said urgently. "I–I can't face her. Knowing that I'll never dance again . . ."

"Of course you'll dance again," Rachel's mother said. "Once you get adjusted to your new routine, you can start ballet classes again. As a matter of fact, Dr. Malar recommends it. Exercise is part of good diabetic control. You can do all the things you did before."

Except eat candy whenever I want. Except live without insulin shots. Except be normal, Rachel thought. She said, "Mom, I don't mind Jenny coming by for a visit. I guess I have to face my friends sooner or later, but not Madame. Please. I–I can't face Madame Pershoff yet."

Mrs. Deering patted Rachel's shoulder. This time Rachel did not jerk away. This time she sat still and swallowed a large lump of sadness that had stuck in her throat. "Maybe later," Rachel said. "After I go home and can go back to the studio and talk to her there. But not here while I'm in the hospital."

"All right, dear. I'll make her understand so she won't come by unexpectedly. Dr. Malar said he'd release you to go home in a couple of days anyway, so there's no need for your friends to visit if you'd rather not have them come here. But why not call Jenny this afternoon when she gets home from school? And Rachel, call Chris, too. She misses you and it would mean a lot to her."

"Sure," Rachel said without much spirit. "I'll call both of them."

When her mother left, Rachel retrieved the diet brochures. She was bending over, scooping them off the floor, when she heard the deep rumble of a male voice. It asked, "Are you Rachel Deering?"

She jerked up and dropped the brochures. The words came from a boy.

Six

" ARE you Rachel Deering?" the boy with
sea-colored eyes asked again. He was
tan and healthy-looking. A cap of dark red
curls clustered and spilled across his forehead.

"Who are you?" Rachel asked, a little
embarrassed to be caught bending over.

"I'm Shawn McLaughlin," the boy said,
entering the room and walking over to her as if
he'd been invited. "Welcome to the wonderful
world of diabetes."

His dancing grin made his eyes crinkle at
the corners. Rachel was a little irritated at his
casual manner. "So who does that make you?
An ambassador of some sort?" she said coolly.

"I'm one of Dr. Malar's patients, like you."

"Are you supposed to make me feel good
about this stupid disease?" Rachel paused, as
if waiting for an answer. "Well, save your
breath. I'll never get used to it."

Shawn lounged against the wall and crossed his arms over his chest. A gold link bracelet around his wrist caught her eye. It sported the Medic Alert medallion. She was becoming more and more irritated by him. How could he just saunter into her room and be so open—almost proud—of his disease? Rachel would just rather keep the whole thing to herself.

"Dr. Malar said you weren't having an easy time of it," Shawn said.

"I hate shots. I hate having my whole life change. I hate this hospital. I hate diabetes—" Rachel began.

"—and you're not too crazy about me, huh?" He finished her outburst for her and then smiled at her brightly.

She felt her cheeks grow warm. "I don't even know you."

"Well, Rachel, I hate shots, too. I've had this crazy disease since I was two. That's twelve years. And at two shots a day for 365 days a year, that's almost 8,800 shots—I'm counting leap years into that total—so I've had to get used to them. But I still hate them."

Rachel stared at him, trying to imagine a huge pile of syringes. Then she gave a half-shrug and turned toward the window. "So why did Dr. Malar send you in here? To comfort me? To let me know I'm not alone?" she said, a bit sarcastically, with a bitter smile.

"Maybe because we're both athletes."

She looked him over carefully. He certainly wasn't a dancer. He didn't have the build for it. "Dominoes?" she ventured, feeling a little friendly in spite of herself.

His grin flashed once more. "Soccer. I started playing when I was six to help control my blood sugar. I know they've told you how diet, exercise, and insulin work together to keep your blood sugar levels under control."

She nodded, recalling bits and pieces of Dr. Malar's and Anne's discussions about managing her illness. Shawn continued. "Anyway, I love the game and play for a team that travels all over the state. I'm the leading scorer on the junior high school squad. I can't wait till next year when I can play high school soccer. Then after that—" He shrugged. "After that, college soccer. With a scholarship, I hope." He paused for a few moments, but Rachel could think of nothing to say. "Dr. Malar says you're a dancer. Are you?"

"I was," she corrected, looking out of the hospital window to a green patch of lawn below. "Ballet. But I'm not sure if I'll still dance."

"Why not?"

She could feel his gaze on her and it

irritated her all over again. What business was it of his anyway? The square of bright green grass began to look wrinkled. Rachel blinked and felt a light-headed feeling all through her body. Without warning, her breath became light and rapid.

"Are you all right?" Shawn's question seemed to come from far away, as if he were talking through a tunnel.

Rachel opened her mouth to answer, but found she couldn't form words. Her knees buckled and Shawn's arm darted around her waist. He said, "Whoa. You'd better sit down."

She let him lead her to a chair in the room, unable to shake the dizzy, spinning sensations. Then she felt a wave of nausea. "Here, eat this." Shawn thrust candy into her hand, and she managed to get it into her mouth. She sucked on it and in a few minutes, the nausea left and the room stopped whirling.

"I–I had no idea candy could be so good for you . . ." she managed weakly.

"Only when you're having an insulin reaction," he told her.

"I read about them." She still felt a little woozy. Shawn poured her some orange juice left over from her breakfast tray and broke open a packet of saltine crackers. "It's a good idea to eat a little something real soon," he said. "To keep your blood sugar level up so you don't have another reaction."

"I thought my blood sugar was supposed to stay low?"

"Never too low. If insulin doesn't have food to work with, you have a reaction. I have to be careful to cover myself with extra food before I play a soccer match. And I always have colas and other sugary drinks with me at the field. If I were you, I'd always carry candy or sugar with me."

She looked at him in shock. "You mean this can happen any time? I might just keel over anywhere?"

"Only if you don't prepare. It's not that scary."

"That's easy for you to say," Rachel mumbled darkly. "I'm never going to get used to all this stuff." She felt like crying, but she couldn't let herself break down in front of this stranger.

"Sure you will. In fact, that's one of the reasons I stopped by. There really are a lot of us diabetics out there. We have a support group. About fifteen of us meet once a month to talk and have fun. We go skating or swimming or we just hang around. It helps. I'd like you to come to our next meeting."

Rachel jumped from the chair and shoved

past Shawn. "No way. I don't even like thinking about my diabetes. I sure don't want to discuss it with a bunch of strangers."

"It helps."

"I said *no*. Are you deaf?"

Shawn shoved his hands into the pockets of his jeans. "I'll keep in touch in case you change your mind."

"Don't bother." She kept her back to him. She didn't see him leave, but could tell when she was alone in the room. She shivered slightly and hugged her arms close to her body. She didn't need Shawn McLaughlin and all his instructions about living with diabetes. It may be true that there was nothing she could do about having it, but she certainly wasn't going to accept it—never.

She leaned her forehead against the clear pane of the window glass and felt sad. And alone, terribly alone.

* * * * *

"I'm surprised you didn't get along better with Shawn. He's got his diabetes in the tightest control of any of my adolescent patients. It's his dedication to sports that makes the difference," Dr. Malar said while Rachel packed her bag to go home.

53

Would her mother never finish with the paperwork downstairs? Rachel only wanted to get out of there. She didn't want to make small talk with her doctor. "Shawn was nice enough," Rachel offered. "But I don't think that support group is for me."

"Your parents will be attending meetings at the Diabetes Research Institute with parents of other diabetics once a month. I was hoping you could make it a family affair."

"I don't think so."

"Research is the key, you know," Dr. Malar ventured. "We're going to find a cure for this disease someday. Do you know that medical teams have already reversed diabetes in dogs? That they've done some transplants of insulin-producing cells into a few humans?"

"Call me when it's my turn," Rachel quipped.

Dr. Malar drummed his fingers on a table top. "If you have any problems, Rachel, any questions at any time, call my office."

"Thanks," she sniffed, trying to ignore him. She knew she'd never call unless her mother made her. All she wanted to do was forget her diabetes. Oh, she'd take her shots and stay on her special diet, but nothing was going to change her mind about accepting what had happened to her.

"You have your blood monitoring equipment and your chemstrips?"

"Yes." Rachel had jammed the machine into the side of her suitcase. With the machine, she could do glucose readings at home with a drop of her blood. This would help her maintain blood sugar levels as close to normal as possible. If she had too high of a reading, she'd have to do some exercising. If she had too low of a reading, she'd have to eat something so as not to face a dreaded insulin reaction. She'd already decided she never wanted to have one of those again!

Dr. Malar said, "For a while, I'll be regulating your insulin dose. But as you grow older and your needs change, you'll decide for yourself. It's *your* illness and you will learn to cope with it. Right now, I want you to go home and resume as normal a life as possible. Do everything you did before—school, dancing, dating."

What would Nick Carter think when he heard? And Melanie? It was too painful to consider, so Rachel shoved aside the memory of their two faces. Then she slammed the lid of her suitcase. "I'll manage," she told Dr. Malar, heaving the piece of luggage off the bed. "Thanks for all your help."

His wise blue eyes looked at her carefully.

"I'll see you in a few weeks in my office for a checkup. Take care."

Rachel let him leave and stood in the middle of the floor staring at the open doorway. The everyday routine sounds of the hospital drifted into her room from the hallway. As much as she wanted to go home, it frightened her to be away from the safety and the security of the hospital, away from her doctors and nurses who helped her with her testing, away from the dieticians who figured out what she could eat. At home and in school, from now on, Rachel Deering knew she was on her own.

Seven

*H*OME. Rachel drifted around her house thinking that it had never looked so good to her. Her bedroom, her four familiar walls, her posters . . . everything looked fresh and sparkling. Her dad had sent a vase of pale pink rosebuds for her dresser. She fingered the petals and sniffed the sweet-smelling buds. Yet as much as things were the same, there were also the subtle reminders of her illness.

Inside her top dresser drawer she'd had to make room for her glucose monitor, her syringes, alcohol swabs, insulin bottles, lancetts for pricking her fingertips, and bottles of testing strips. There was even a large package of roll candy for her to carry in her purse.

Rachel wandered down the hall, drifted into the kitchen, and opened the refrigerator door. Even the contents of the refrigerator had been changed to reflect her new lifestyle. Two unopened boxes of insulin, lots of protein foods, fresh fruit and non-caloric beverages filled the shelves, which had once held leftover cake and other sugary goodies. She felt guilty because her whole family would have to adjust to her new eating habits. "It'll do us good," her dad had said, but Rachel knew the truth. Her diabetes was changing everybody's life.

"I missed you," Chris said shyly as Rachel shut the refrigerator door, juggling an apple, a wedge of cheese, and a diet soft drink. She sat at the table trying not to drool over Chris' mound of cookies and tall glass of ice-cold milk.

"I'm glad to be home. The hospital's a real drag. So what's new?" Even though Rachel hated to admit it, she *had* missed the little kid.

"Madame Pershoff is letting me be in the concert this Christmas," Chris beamed. "I did a combination like she wanted, perfect! I didn't mess up once and so she said I could be in the corps of dancers."

The concert! Rachel had almost forgotten about it.

Chris spoke with her mouth full of cookies. "Aren't you going to dance class this afternoon? Madame Pershoff was asking about you."

Rachel gulped down a swallow of soda,

dreading seeing her ballet instructor. But she knew that she'd have to face her sooner or later. "I guess I will," Rachel told Chris. "Not to dance or anything. But maybe I'll just stop by the studio and say hi to everybody."

"Good. We're all working really hard to get ready for the concert. You sure got a lot of catching up to do. Gosh, it's only nine weeks away." Chris' eyes grew wide.

"I know," Rachel said. "I can count. Chris, do you have to slurp your milk? And do you have to dunk the cookies? It looks so disgusting."

"Well excuse me," Chris huffed, jutting her lower lip out in a pout. "I was just reminding you."

"The last thing I need is reminding."

"Aren't you going to try for the part of the Swan solo?" Chris' eyes widened as she waited for the answer.

"I'm not sure. I don't know what I want to do . . ." The ringing of the telephone interrupted her.

"Welcome home!" Jenny said cheerfully. "I can't wait to see you. How are you doing?"

Rachel wrapped the phone cord around her finger and lounged against the countertop. "I'm doing fine."

"Are you going to be in school on Monday?

I've got a zillion things to tell you."

"I'll be there." Rachel talked to Jenny as long as she could, hoping that it would make her too late to go to the studio. But her mother's impatient glare made her wrap up her conversation.

Rachel kept quiet during the ride to the studio. She was dreading the visit more than she even imagined. The old stucco building looked dingy and worn out from the street. Its paint was flaking and peeling in the hot Miami sun. Even in October, there wasn't much relief from the heat. Rachel climbed the long flight of stairs to the second floor studio. The climb seemed endless.

In the studio, the old familiar smells and sounds gave her a lump in her throat. The tinny notes of the piano and the scents of perspiration and rosin and dust smelled a bit like a school gymnasium. But the smell of hairspray and lemon air freshener gave it a unique smell that tugged at Rachel's heart.

She stood at the door and stared into the vast studio. At the barre, her advanced classmates worked and stretched in black leotards, their legs set off in pale pink tights. She heard the soft swish of ballet slippers sweep across the wooden floor.

She wanted to join them at the barre, but

she couldn't bring herself to walk out of the doorway. Several girls caught her reflection in the mirror. A few looked toward her. They know, she told herself. They all know I'm sick.

"Rachel, dear!" Rachel's thoughts were interrupted by the sharp greeting from Madame Pershoff. Rachel watched the older woman come toward her, her cane tapping a quick rhythm. "Come into my office, dear. We must talk." The accent was as thick and distinct as ever.

Meekly, Rachel followed Madame Pershoff into her office, which was a cubby hole with a rumbling old air conditioner. The walls were covered with aged black and white photos of Madame when she was younger, in gorgeous, classical ballet dresses.

"Sit down," Madame commanded, sweeping a sleeping cat off an old leather sofa. She settled directly across from the sofa in her old swivel desk chair. "How good to see you. Oh, we have missed you so much, Rachel. And we're so sorry for this terrible thing that has happened to you."

Rachel smiled weakly, a bit taken aback by Madame's kind greeting. She hadn't expected it. "It's good to be back."

"You look very good now, not like you did weeks ago. You were so sick," Madame

Pershoff said gently. "But that is behind you. Now you are back and there is much work for you to do to get into shape. The concert is only weeks away."

"I won't be dancing in the concert, Madame," Rachel said. She twisted her hands in her lap and took a deep breath and plunged ahead. "I–I've missed too much to compete for the solo. No matter how hard I work, I can't compete this year."

"It's true that you've missed classes, but with hard work . . ."

"No. I–I can't." How could Rachel ever explain her fears about insulin reactions? How could she ever make Madame understand how radically changed her life was now?

"But you love to dance!"

The words made Rachel's eyes fill with tears. Quickly, she turned her head and stared at the floor. The drab olive carpet looked worn and needed vacuuming. "I'll always love to dance. With all my heart."

Madame Pershoff's cane thudded resoundingly on the rug. "Then you must not give up your love. Or your dreams. Look at you. You still have the dancer's body and carriage. You still have two legs that work." Rachel knew that Madame's own legs had been stiffened by arthritis. "You know you can do it. Your doctor encouraged you to resume dancing, didn't he?"

"Yes."

"Then you must do it." Why couldn't Rachel make Madame understand it wasn't so simple? Madame Pershoff continued. "I have many students. Some are good. A few are very good."

"Like Melanie?"

Madame Pershoff raised her eyebrows, and her dark piercing eyes looked straight into Rachel's. "She *is* technically good, Rachel. That is important. Skill is necessary. But you, Rachel . . . ah! You have the heart for the dance, the spirit and soul for it. This is a gift one is born with. One cannot learn it no matter how many years one practices. Do you know what I am telling you?"

"I think so . . ." Rachel was a little confused. She'd never had Madame talk so encouragingly to her. There'd been a time when it would have made her walk on air. But now, all she felt was confusion. Diabetes had messed up her life, moved into her body like an alien, and become an unwelcome part of her. She was a puppet at its command. It said: "Eat this. Don't eat this. Get your shot. Beware of reactions."

Abruptly, Rachel stood. "Thank you for being so nice to me, Madame Pershoff. I appreciate all you're doing to help me."

"Come back to class, Rachel," the silver-haired woman urged. "The Christmas concert is not important for you. I will give the part to Melanie. But there will be other concerts, other parts. Start back with exercises and barre work. I feel you have a future in dance. Please, do not give up."

Rachel backed out of the office and hurried to the stairwell. She passed through the studio, looking away from the members of the class. She knew she was about to cry and couldn't stand the thought of them seeing her break down. She paused momentarily at the doorway, glancing over her shoulder in time to watch Melanie rise on pointe and execute a perfect arabesque.

Melanie was so healthy! She had a perfect dancer's body, healthy and well, just ready to fulfill her dreams. With a sob clawing to get out of her, Rachel hurdled down the stairs, two at a time, into the blinding Miami sunlight.

Eight

ON Monday morning, Rachel walked through the halls at school, trying not to be noticed. She'd been away for ten class days, and coming back wasn't easy for her. It seemed like everybody was whispering about her.

Then there was the bother of having to duck into the girls' bathroom and hide in a stall in order to eat a mid-morning snack. Since her lunch break was so late in the day, she didn't want to run the risk of having a reaction. She also found that the combination of higher blood sugars and nerves made her need to use the bathroom more often. By the time she entered the cafeteria for lunch, Rachel felt jittery and jumpy.

"Hey, Rachel! Come sit with me and Ben." Jenny's invitation greeted Rachel as she emerged from the cashier's table, lunch tray in her hands. Rachel plopped her tray down next to her friend. Jenny asked, "So, how are you doing?"

"All right."

"Did you see the weird hairdo Paige Williams has? I mean really weird!" Jenny gossiped over the hubbub of the cafeteria.

"I can't say that I have," Rachel said as she sipped her milk. She let her eyes wander around the room while Jenny went into detail about Paige's hairstyle. At the far end of the table, her gaze stopped on Nick Carter sitting with his friends.

She remembered the day he'd helped her to the clinic. Had she ever thanked him? Her memory was fuzzy. She was only able to remember how bad she'd felt and how strong his arms had been as he supported her. If only she had the courage to go over and talk to him. If only she was more like Jenny. Jenny was so outgoing and clever. She swallowed hard imagining the conversation she might have with him. But she lost her chance as he left the cafeteria with two other guys. They were laughing and Nick never once looked backward. Rachel fought her disappointment. Why bother? she told herself. Nick doesn't even know I'm alive.

"Hey, Rachel." Jenny's voice intruded into

her thoughts. "Why is that cute guy in the lunch line waving at you?"

Rachel snapped her attention to where Jenny pointed, and her mouth dropped open in amazement. There stood Shawn McLaughlin, grinning at her, his curly red hair spilling onto his forehead. Panic grabbed her as he advanced toward her table. Of all the people to run into! Why did it have to be someone to remind her of her diabetes?

"Hi," he said as he approached her. "I thought that was you. How's it going?"

"Hi," she managed stiffly. "What are you doing here?"

"Our school's soccer team is playing yours after school today. Didn't you know?"

Vaguely, she remembered hearing something about it over the speakers during morning announcements. "Well, of course . . ."

"You are coming to cheer me on, aren't you?" His eyes twinkled at her.

Jenny stared at them both and Rachel's cheeks began to burn. "I don't think so."

"Too bad," he said. "We're going to win big."

"I'm not into soccer," Rachel said lamely.

Jenny cleared her throat. Rachel started. "Oh, uh—Shawn, uh—this is my friend Jenny."

Jenny smiled, showing her dimples. "So where has Rachel been keeping you?"

Rachel was so embarrassed. This is one time that she didn't need Jenny's openness. Shawn shrugged. "We met in the hospital. Didn't she tell you?"

"Not a word," Jenny answered.

Rachel wished she could slide under the table. Just when she had almost forgotten about her diabetes and was with her "normal" friends, Shawn McLaughlin had to turn up and remind her all over again how different she was. "I've been very busy getting back into the swing of things," she said slowly.

"We're having a support group meeting this Sunday. You coming?"

Never! Rachel said to herself silently. Then, calmly, her voice said, "I'm busy."

"Support group? What's a support group?" Jenny quizzed.

Abruptly, Rachel stood and gathered her things. "Look, I've got to run. I don't want to be late for class."

Shawn wrinkled his brow. "Sure you won't change your mind about today's game?"

"Yeah, Rachel. Ben and I are going. Where's your school spirit? We can't let these guys beat the old gold and blue without a few cheers, can we?" Jenny said enthusiastically. "We could all sit together," she added.

"No," Rachel said firmly and headed for the door.

"Too bad," Shawn called after her. "It's going to be great!"

By the time Rachel had escaped into the sunlight, she was fuming. To her, Shawn McLaughlin was a conceited creep, even if he was good-looking and athletic. He had no right to come over and embarrass her in front of her friends. And he had no right to ask about the stupid support group and remind her of all the things she wanted to forget.

"Wait up!" Jenny called, walking swiftly to Rachel's side. "Want to tell me what's going on here?"

Rachel shivered in the slight nip of the November air. "What's going on where?"

"Don't be cute," Jenny said. "Why didn't you mention this guy before? How did you meet him in the hospital?"

Rachel took a deep breath. "He has diabetes, too. My doctor sent him in to advise me. Because he's in such perfect control and because he's so *perfect* all the way around." She said the last part with meanness in her voice. "I don't like him very much."

"Well, I think he likes you."

"Oh, come on. That's silly."

"No. I could tell by the way he was looking at you. He's definitely interested," Jenny insisted.

"No way. He's just trying to lure me into that dumb support group. Between him and my parents, that's all I hear." She mimicked her mother's voice. " 'Now, Rachel. You really should attend the group meeting. Be with other kids your age with the same problems.' "

"So what's so terrible about that?" Jenny's wide-eyed gaze reflected genuine curiosity.

"Jenny, please. There's no way to explain it. I just don't want to be around them. I don't want to be near 'kids like me.' "

"But you hang around with other dancers. What's wrong with being around kids with diabetes?"

Rachel felt exasperated with Jenny. She just didn't understand. "Just forget it!" She threw up her hands in resignation. "I've got plenty of things going on right now."

"But you're not dancing in the Christmas concert. You're not even taking classes right now."

"I'm still adjusting."

Jenny reasoned, "Okay. So forget the other stuff. Come to the game with Ben and me. It'll be fun to watch this guy play. I mean, there's no one else in your life."

70

Rachel thought about Nick Carter briefly. Then she clamped her mouth into a firm line. "I don't care, cute or not. I just don't like Shawn McLaughlin and I don't want to be around him. Now please stop bothering me about it!" Rachel spun on her heel and stalked off toward her next class.

* * * * *

Spitballs whizzed over Rachel's head in the choral room where the noise from ninety-three kids—seventh through ninth grades—was deafening. Rachel was relieved to be in the final class of her day. She ignored the racket and thumbed through the Christmas holiday sheet music.

The Christmas music made her realize how different her Christmas was going to be this year. Imagine getting up and having to give herself a shot before even opening her gifts! And no more candied sweet potatoes or pumpkin pies or her mom's special sugar-dipped figs either. She folded the music glumly.

Miss Hoggard came through the doorway yelling, "Quiet!" Immediately, the room calmed down. "That's better," she said. "All right, let's turn to page four in your booklets, measure two." Papers rustled. "Sopranos, you're in first. Then the altos, followed by you tenors and basses. And basses," she added with irritation, "you're at least four beats off. Pay attention."

The piano began the familiar melody and Rachel peered down at her soprano line. The piano sounded strange and far away to Rachel's ears. The sheet music fluttered in her hands. She tried to control the shaking and trembling of her hands, but couldn't. She felt terribly weak. Her breath came quickly and rapidly.

"Are you okay?" Diane, who sat next to her, asked. "You look really pale."

Horrified, Rachel knew what was happening to her. She was having an insulin reaction. She'd been distracted by Shawn's appearance and hadn't eaten enough lunch. "M–My purse," she managed to mumble through white, trembling lips. "In my purse . . . . Candy . . ."

By this time, the entire soprano section knew something was wrong. Heads began to turn and eyes began to zero in on her.

"Girls!" Miss Hoggard snapped. "Why the talking? What is going on up there?" She strained her neck to see the top rows, her lips caught in a tight frown.

Diane handed Rachel her purse and explained, "Rachel Deering doesn't feel well. I think she's sick."

"Well, then go to the clinic, Rachel. I have a class to conduct."

Rachel fumbled with the clasp on her purse, her hands shaking so much that she could barely control them. Silently, she begged, Don't let me pass out. She located the roll of candy, tore off three at once, and shoved them into her mouth. She sucked on them until the nausea disappeared and the awful trembling stopped.

The room stopped spinning, and Rachel became aware of all eyes on her. She felt humiliated. Miss Hoggard tapped her reed-thin director's baton on her music stand and asked, "Are you going to be all right?" Her tone was cross.

"Yes," Rachel mumbled, fighting down tears. "I'm okay now."

"Then may we return to the music?"

The pianist resumed playing. The choir members slowly refocused their attention on the music. Rachel sat still in her chair, wishing she could die, absolutely die. She'd never been more embarrassed in her life. All she wanted to do was go home and away from her diabetes forever.

Nine

"I won't go! I'm telling you, I simply won't go!" After her angry announcement, Rachel ran into her bedroom, slammed the door, and threw herself across her bed.

"Open this door this instant, young lady!" Mrs. Deering demanded, rapping on the door. Rachel jerked her pillow over her head and hoped her mother would go away. "I mean it, Rachel. Right now!" The knocking continued until Rachel got up and let her mother into her room. "What is the meaning of this tantrum of yours?"

"I told you. I don't want to go," Rachel fumed.

"Well, I'm telling you that you're going. Madame Pershoff has given Chris a role in the concert and our whole family is going to watch her perform. And that means *you*, too."

How could her parents be so unfair? Rachel

fumed. Didn't they know how hard it would be for her to sit through the concert? To watch her friends dancing? To see Melanie dance the part she'd so desperately wanted? It was all Madame Pershoff's fault. Why did she choose her dumb sister for a part anyway?

"It's hard to sit and watch," Rachel said glumly.

"I understand that." Mrs. Deering settled on the bed while Rachel paced the floor. "But you're the one who decided to quit dancing. We've all encouraged you to return. Even Dr. Malar thinks it's the best thing for your diabetic control."

Her diabetic control. It always came back to that. But no one in her family had ever suffered through an insulin reaction. Ever since that time in chorus weeks before, Rachel lived in fear of having another one. How could she dance wondering if she would keel over in class, or worse, during a stage performance?

"I plan to go back to class," Rachel hedged. "Right after the holidays. I want to start back slowly. Diabetes is a big adjustment, you know."

"Don't you think your father and I know that? Don't you think I'd trade places with you in a minute if I could?" The look on her mother's face made Rachel believe her. "I

75

know how miserable it is to have your whole life turned upside down. But you're only thirteen . . ."

"Almost fourteen," Rachel corrected.

"The point is—you can't crawl into a hole and disappear. You have your entire life ahead of you."

Rachel admitted that that much was true. Her life stretched before her in a long line of needles and insulin bottles. Mrs. Deering continued when Rachel didn't respond, "You know, your dad and I have made good friends with the McLaughlin family through the parental support group. The meetings are fascinating and so much progress is being made in the area of research. And their son, Shawn, is very nice. I know he's asked you to join them in their young people's support group."

Rachel glared at her mother. "Can we get off this topic, Mom? I don't want to sit around comparing notes on my illness with a bunch of sick kids. I don't like to think of myself as sick."

"You're not sick, Rachel." Mrs. Deering said. "But you do have a serious medical condition, and it helps to face it and deal with it. Ignoring it won't make it go away."

Rachel made a face at her mother. "I'm not ignoring it. It won't let me."

Mrs. Deering let out a long sigh before rising from the bed. "Well, everybody needs help at one time or another, but I won't nag you into doing anything you don't want to do, as long as you continue to take care of yourself. Now, please get dressed. The concert starts in two hours and Chris has to be backstage in an hour. I won't have your attitude interfere with your sister's big evening."

She made it to the door before Rachel said, "I'll go. I know how important it is to Chris. It used to be important to me, too. But, Mom, please do me one favor."

"I'll try."

"Please stop talking about the *Great* Shawn McLaughlin. I'm sick of hearing his name."

"Okay," her mother said, then left the room, closing the door behind her.

* * * * *

The grand old Olympus Theater had the graceful interior and stone arches of 1930s architecture. Rachel slouched in a deeply padded seat, staring at the massive red velvet curtain hanging across the stage. The curtain was highlighted by strategically placed spotlights.

People drifted down the plushly carpeted aisle, dressed in their festive best. A huge chandelier glimmered down from the center of the elaborately hand-painted ceiling.

As quiet and calm as things were in front of the stage, Rachel knew how chaotic the activity would be behind the curtain. Dancers would be stretching on chairs which acted as makeshift barres. Dressing rooms would be a clutter of satin, feathers, and sequins. Tables would be littered with greasepaint makeup. Pointe shoes with long satin ribbons would be spilling out of duffle bags and carryall boxes.

Dancers, frantic with stage fright, would be huddled in groups, some in tears, some in excited anticipation. In all her years as a dancer, this was the first time Rachel Deering was not a part of the pre-concert scene. It was more than she could bear. She twisted around in her seat. Her father was in the lobby and her mother was backstage with Chris. Then she saw Nick Carter lounging against a stone pillar. Naturally, he was there to watch Melanie in her triumphant moment as solo ballerina. The lights dimmed, and she lost sight of Nick. When the stage lit up and the curtain rose, she became lost in the music and beauty of the ballet in spite of herself. Then Melanie entered. Even Rachel gasped over her flawless performance. When the curtain came down on the final number, Rachel clapped enthusiastically with the rest of the audience.

After the performance she went backstage. The dancers were fluttering around, squealing in delight and relief. They reminded Rachel of tiny butterflies. Here and there, excited relatives flashed cameras at some of the dancers.

"Did you see me, Mom? Rachel? What did you think?" Chris barreled up to Rachel and Mrs. Deering, talking in breathless spurts. "Wasn't it fabulous?"

"Fabulous," Mrs. Deering beamed.

"You did very well," Rachel added, watching Melanie, who was still in costume, holding hands with Nick. She was cradling a cluster of red roses. Rachel knew they were from Madame Pershoff. Madame always gave flowers to her lead dancer. A twinge twisted in Rachel like a turning knife. She suddenly wanted to get out of there!

"Rachel, Mrs. Deering . . . please, there is someone I want you to meet." The sound of Madame's voice made Rachel turn. Madame Pershoff was coming toward her, her silver-headed cane bumping the floor decisively. A tall man with a distinctive mane of thick white hair and the unmistakable carriage of a dancer, walked next to her. Somehow, the man looked familiar to Rachel.

"This is Michael Tolavitch. We once danced together in Europe. Now Michael is with the New York City Ballet as instructor and choreographer." Of course! Rachel remembered seeing him in the photographs on Madame's wall.

"Pleased to meet you." His voice was deep as he gave Rachel a long hard look. "Tasha tells me that you did not dance tonight because you've been ill. That's too bad. She speaks highly of your talent. I would like to have seen you perform."

Rachel wondered if her own eyes were as saucer-round as Chris' had been. "Thank you," she said.

He walked around her slowly, looking at her critically. "Yes. You have the form and carriage. Your head sits well and your neck is very long. And your height is perfect! We have few girls in our company below five-foot-five. A dancer must be tall and elegant."

Rachel could scarcely believe her ears. Such encouragement from a man of this caliber in the world of dance! If only she could have danced for him . . .

"I plan to return in the spring, Rachel. Perhaps you will be well enough to dance for me then." He smiled a dazzling smile at her and clasped her hand warmly before turning away to survey other dancers.

Madame Pershoff broke into effusive speech. "I knew he would like you, Rachel." She leaned closer, as if to conspire with Rachel. "Now here is the best news. Michael will be returning in May for the Southeast Regional Auditions. Dancers will be selected for full scholarships to study this summer with the School of American Ballet of the New York City Ballet. Think of it!

"I have only a few students I would consider for such a competition—Melanie, Patricia, and you. But you must come back to classes as soon as possible to get ready for the auditions. Think of it, Rachel! Wouldn't it be worth all the work?"

Speechless, Rachel nodded.

* * * * *

Christmas tree lights blinked off and on, colorful dashes of artificial light glimmering in the darkened living room. Rachel lay stretched out on the floor in front of the tree. The smell of pine was in the air. Gifts, wrapped and waiting for Christmas Day, were clustered beneath the tree.

Rachel rested her chin on her palms, thinking about the recent events of her life.

The New York City Ballet. There was a time when she'd have moved heaven and earth to attend those auditions. Yet, how could she when diabetes haunted her life? She couldn't escape it.

"What are you doing in the dark?" Chris padded across the carpet uninvited and sat cross-legged on the floor beside her sister.

"Wishing for my fairy godmother to come along."

"Surprise," Chris said, grinning. "Here I am."

"I really would like to be alone."

Chris ignored the request. "Wasn't tonight wonderful, Rachel? Lucky you. Being asked to go to the regional auditions by Mr. Tolavitch. I hope I get asked someday. Are you going to go?"

"He didn't ask me, Chris," Rachel corrected with irritation. "He simply said he'd like to see me dance someday."

"But Madame said—"

"Madame Pershoff is interested in building up the reputation of her school," Rachel interrupted. "Of course I'd like to go. If it weren't for my diabetes—"

"Oh, pooh!" Chris dismissed Rachel's excuse with a flip of her hand. "People get diabetes all the time and still do the things they want to do. You can work hard and go to the auditions . . ."

Rachel sat upright. "What do you know about it? You don't know anything. So keep your opinions to yourself."

"I know plenty," Chris sputtered. "I know that you haven't been fit to live with since you came home from the hospital."

"Well, it didn't happen to you, smarty."

"So what? I'm sorry you're sick and I'm not. Okay? I'm sorry you have to get shots every day and I don't. Does that make you feel any better?"

"Oh, hush up and go away. You don't know anything."

"You bet I'll go away," Chris said, rising to her feet, tears springing to her small eyes. "But I do too know something! You're nothing but a big fat coward. You're just a quitter! Do you know that? A quitter!"

Chris ran from the room and Rachel stared after her, her mouth open in shock. A sudden haze of tears misted her eyes, making the tree lights shimmer as if a film of rain had landed on cold, hard glass.

Ten

"NICE haul, Rachel." The comment came from Jenny as she fingered her friend's gifts the Saturday following Christmas Day.

"Yeah, it is, isn't it?"

"Did I show you the bracelet Ben got me?" Jenny held out her wrist and showed off a thin gold chain.

"About twenty times. I told you it was beautiful." Rachel meant it, but she did feel a little jealous.

"Phone call, Rachel." Mrs. Deering's voice shouted from the kitchen.

Rachel picked up the extension in the hallway.

"How'd you like to watch me do my stuff on the soccer field?" It was Shawn McLaughlin. Rachel's fist tightened around the receiver. Jenny followed her into the hallway and mouthed, "Who is it?"

"Uh—hi, Shawn," Rachel said. "Soccer game? When?"

"We'll pick you up at ten. The game's at eleven and it lasts about two hours. Then we'll grab lunch at a burger place."

"Well, I–I don't know . . ."

Jenny tugged at Rachel's shirttail and whispered, "Go on! Go for it!"

"It'll be a good match," Shawn continued.

Rachel was caught in the middle of Jenny's dramatics and Shawn's offer and she felt flustered. She didn't even *like* Shawn McLaughlin! "I–I guess I could go . . ." she heard her voice say.

"Good. I'll pick you up in an hour."

She hung up and listened to Jenny's gleeful applause. "Hey! You got a date. Let's go get you dressed. Something new . . . maybe that red sweater with your jeans . . ."

Rachel walked after her into the bedroom. "Now hold on, Jenny. It's hardly a date. Some other girl probably canceled out on him."

"Wow, aren't you the party pooper. Didn't it occur to you that Shawn wants to take *you*?"

"At the last minute?"

"Ben never does anything until the last minute. Stop talking the guy down. He's cute and you know it, Rachel."

"But I don't like him." Rachel crossed her arms in front of her.

Jenny eyed her skeptically. "The heck you don't, Rachel Deering. If you really didn't like him, you wouldn't get so wound up every time someone mentions his name."

"I do not!"

Jenny arched her eyebrow. "Then why are you standing there sputtering instead of getting ready? If you really thought he was a creep, you'd have hung up on him."

"I agreed to go just to get you and my mother off my case." Rachel felt color seep into her cheeks.

"Why can't you admit that you think the guy's cool, but you're afraid to go out with him?"

"Afraid? Of what?"

"Of liking a guy who has no hang-ups over his diabetes." Rachel's back stiffened, but she couldn't think of anything to say. Jenny held up the bright red sweater that still smelled new from the store. "Now put this on. Your date will be here in forty minutes."

* * * * *

The sun was bright, but the air was chilly. Rachel huddled in her ski jacket on the bleachers at the side of the field, watching Shawn and his teammates go through their warm-up paces. First, they stretched their legs. She was surprised that they used many of the same stretching exercises that she did as a dancer.

Shawn looked strong in his soccer uniform. His uniform was black and consisted of shorts, shirt, and socks. "For the Blackwatch," he'd told her in the car on the way to the field. "It's a crack military unit in Scotland that started back in the sixteenth century." She watched him fire a practice ball at the net and the goalie dive to push it out. Although she knew nothing about soccer, she could tell Shawn was good at it. By the time the referee blew the whistle to start the game, she'd forgotten how cold she was.

The game was fast—electrically fast. She soon got caught up in it. She even stood to yell when the Blackwatch scored late in the first half. But it wasn't until it was almost over that she realized how strenuous the game of soccer must be. But Shawn played effortlessly. If he was afraid of insulin reactions, he didn't show it. Nervously, she chewed her lip. She was almost afraid that he'd keel over with a reaction, but at the same time she was amazed by the intensity of his play on the field.

When the final whistle sounded and the Blackwatch had won by two goals, Rachel decided she would ask him about it. How could he play so hard, and still be a diabetic? In the burger place, with the sun streaming through a row of windows and Shawn wolfing down a double cheeseburger, a shake, and double fries, Rachel asked him. "So how come you don't have a reaction out on the field?"

He paused before bringing a handful of fries to his mouth. "I prepare for the game by timing my meals and having sugar drinks available on the sidelines."

"And you've never had a reaction during a game?"

"Nope."

Grudgingly, she watched him eat food that was forbidden to her. "I wish I could have a milkshake."

"You could," he countered. "If you worked out as hard as I do in a soccer match."

"Dancing takes a lot of energy," she said.

"Then after a workout, you should be able to have a milkshake."

She rolled her shoulders, annoyed that he made it seem so simple. He seemed to be saying, "Be a good girl and dance hard and you, too, can have goodies to eat." She felt herself resenting him again.

"Look," Shawn said, leaning back against the smooth wood of the booth, hooking his elbows over the top edge. "Your diabetes is a fact of life. You can either control it, or let it control you."

She looked at him with a frown. She'd been having a good time until now. Why was he acting so superior about diabetes? "Do you have a degree in medicine? You're so free with your advice about how I should act."

"I don't have a degree. But I've had diabetes a long time. I thought some of my experiences might help you out. In spite of herself, Rachel felt herself go soft at his friendly grin. "Do you think you're the only one who hates having diabetes?" Shawn continued.

"You don't seem to mind."

"I can't change it," he clarified. "But I do mind."

"I mind, too," Rachel confessed, lacing her fingers together and staring down at them.

"Come to a support group meeting with me," he asked, hunching forward across the table.

She felt as if he'd smacked her. "Is that why you asked me to your game today?" Rachel felt hostile all over again. "To tell me about those stupid meetings again?"

He tipped his head to one side, his aqua-blue eyes sparkling in the warm sunlight. "I asked you because I think you're pretty and I wanted to show you off."

His answer made her mind turn to mush. No one had ever called her pretty before. Rachel felt her cheeks grow warm. She couldn't think of anything to say.

"Tomorrow is a skating party," Shawn was saying. "Our group does some activity once a month and this time around, it's skating. Afterward, we'll go back to Molly Levine's house for hot dogs and maybe a movie on the VCR. Why don't you come with me?"

"Skating . . ." Rachel managed to say. "It might be fun . . ."

"Good. I'll pick you up at three."

Rachel could only nod. Her tongue felt glued to the roof of her mouth. Shawn took her hand and led her out of the restaurant. She followed, her emotions in confusion. Somehow, she didn't dislike him anymore, not in the least. In fact, he made her pulse race faster than Nick Carter ever had. To her shock, she knew she was falling for him like a lead weight.

*　*　*　*　*

That afternoon, Rachel climbed the stairs to the rehearsal studio and peered inside. She heard the familiar strains of piano music and the hard rapping of Madame Pershoff's cane against the floor.

A class of younger girls worked at the barre. Rachel watched with determined fascination. She *did* want to dance again, more than anything. Her fears were slowly being chased away by her desire to dance.

Madame Pershoff noticed her near the end of class. After the class was dismissed, she came over, leaning heavily on the cane for support. "It's good to see you again, Rachel."

"It's good to be back, Madame."

"*Are* you back, Rachel?" Madame Pershoff asked, pointedly.

Rachel raised her chin. "Yes. I want to start work as soon as I can. I want to be ready for the dance scholarship competitions with Mr. Tolavitch."

"You've been out a long time, Rachel. It won't be easy to regain your former condition. Are you willing to work harder than ever before in your life?"

"I am."

"Good. Because I want to take you to those auditions. You have the makings of a very fine dancer. Your future depends on how much you want it. And on how hard you're willing to work for it."

Eleven

THE skating party was nothing like Rachel thought it would be—boring and filled with kids who talked about diets and problems with their diabetes. The kids from Shawn's support group were average, normal kids who seemed pleased to have her along. As they blended into the crowd at the skating rink, Rachel soon forgot that she was doing something with "sick" people. Instead, she just had a good time with Shawn and the rest of the kids.

Molly Levine reminded her of Jenny, always clowning around. Another girl, Lynn, seemed shy. She kept staring adoringly at Shawn. It didn't take Rachel very long to figure out that Lynn had a king-sized crush on him.

"Having a good time?" Shawn asked when they sat down for a drink in the snack bar adjoining the rink.

"Yes, I am," Rachel admitted truthfully. "Where do we go from here?"

"Back to Molly's."

"Is that when we all discuss our problems?"

"We talk. But a person only shares if he feels like it."

"So I can sit and listen?" Rachel asked.

"I thought you liked to talk!" Shawn teased. "Do you think you *can* just sit and listen?" he continued with a smile.

She grinned back at him. "That's all I want to do for the first time."

"Then that's all you have to do."

She stirred her straw around in the cup, watching the liquid create a small whirlpool. "I went back to the studio and told Madame Pershoff I'd be starting classes up again."

"Good for you!"

Rachel felt proud of her decision. "I might not have if I hadn't watched you in that soccer game." Then her tone grew shy. "It was a real eye-opener. I mean, seeing how hard you worked out. It made me miss dance."

He tipped his head to one side and she saw furrows of concentration form along his brow. "I believe that a person can do anything he sets his mind on doing. Diabetes may be a handicap, but it's not the end of the world."

"I thought so three months ago."

"And what do you think now?"

"And now, I just want to get on with life. I want to start training for a dance scholarship competition in May. If I can win one, then I can spend the summer in New York studying with one of the top dance companies in the country."

Shawn studied her briefly. "Is that what you want with all your heart?"

"With all my heart," she said firmly.

He reached across the table and folded his hands around hers, pulled her up on her skates where the carpeted floor gave them a non-skid footing. "Then go for it," he urged.

He drew Rachel to his side, to the hollow of his arm. She stared into his soft eyes. They glided onto the rink, swept up into the mass of spinning skaters and the beat of flowing music. It was impossible for them to speak, but for Rachel, it didn't matter. She was suddenly tongue-tied, unable to say anything to him. She was just realizing how much she was starting to care for Shawn McLaughlin.

* * * * *

Rachel's days became a blur. She was up at six for exercises, breakfast, and an insulin shot. Then there was school followed by dance classes. Next was dinner, an insulin shot, and homework. On Saturdays, there were more hours of dance classes. She took Sundays off at Madame Pershoff's insistence and attended the diabetes support group. There she saw Shawn and listened to kids her age share their problems.

Openly, one had commented, "Just once I'd like to pig out on a hot fudge sundae and *not* feel guilty."

"Yeah. Too bad guilt doesn't stop you though," another said.

Everyone had laughed understandingly and Rachel knew exactly how they felt. She too, had "sneaked" more than one forbidden treat.

Rachel made an extra effort to get along with Chris. Rachel knew that Chris didn't eat sweets and snacks just to get to Rachel. But it still irritated her some.

Shawn sometimes called, but he didn't ask Rachel out again. As spring returned to Miami and the mild winter gave way to the muggy days of April, Rachel realized she was getting back in shape. But she was losing her relationship with Shawn in the process.

The competitions were only a month away and school was winding down for the year. Rachel shared her feelings about Shawn with Jenny late one Sunday afternoon.

"I just think he's giving you lots of space to get back into shape," Jenny observed from her stretched out position on the floor of Rachel's bedroom. "I mean, Shawn knows how important this competition is to you. And isn't he busy with all his soccer stuff, too?"

Rachel shrugged. "Sure, he's busy. His Blackwatch team is playing in State Cup. That's some sort of contest to decide who's got the best team in Florida. He's been traveling a lot."

"So there's your answer," Jenny said with a smile. "He hasn't had the time to date. And you haven't either."

"Or the interest," Rachel added glumly.

"I have an idea!" Jenny snapped her fingers and sat upright. "The Spring Fling Dance is coming up in a week. Ben and I are going. Why don't you ask Shawn to come with you?"

Rachel looked at her friend in surprise. "I can't do that! I've never asked a boy for a date."

"So what? There's always a first time. And besides, you're not going with anyone else, are you?"

"Of course not." Rachel recalled that days before, Melanie had bragged about going with Nick as they'd changed for dance class. At the time, it hadn't even fazed her. She had been totally engrossed in preparing for the competition. And she hadn't thought about Nick Carter in a romantic way for months.

"Just think," Jenny continued in an excited burst. "We could double date. Oh, Rachel! It'd be so much fun!"

Rachel's palms began to sweat as she turned the idea over in her mind. To spend a whole evening with Shawn. To dance with him, be with him . . . "I'll think about it."

"The heck you will," Jenny said, standing and hauling Rachel to her feet. "Go call him right now." She pushed Rachel gently out of the doorway, toward the hall phone.

"Oh, I couldn't, Jenny. I–I have to think about it."

"Why? Do you want to go or not?"

Rachel chewed her bottom lip, thinking about the fun the four of them might have. "You're right," she said with determination. "All he can say is no. I'll do it." She picked up the phone and took a deep breath. How did boys ever get the nerve to ask for a date? She swallowed hard and punched his number. What if he did say no? Worse yet, what if he laughed at her?

Jenny poked her in the ribs. "Is it ringing?"

"Yes," Rachel answered quietly. "Maybe he isn't—"

"Hello," Shawn answered.

"Hi, there," Rachel said, trying to sound nonchalant. "It's me, Rachel." To herself, she added, What a dumb way to start off.

"Oh, hi."

He certainly didn't seem too excited about hearing her voice. A short silence stretched between them. "What are you doing?" Rachel asked, stalling for time.

"Homework. I've got a term paper due tomorrow," he answered. Then there was more silence.

"I called because, well, I was wondering if maybe . . . I mean, our school is having a dance next Saturday night and I thought you might like to come with me . . . and my friends Jenny and Ben . . ."

"Say that again," he asked.

Rachel felt her face flush and almost dropped the receiver. He wanted her to say it again! "I said, our school is having a dance next Saturday night and would you like to double with my friends Jenny and Ben?"

"Sure."

"What? You would?"

"Sure. I'd like to go very much."

"Well, gee . . . that's great . . ."

"We can talk about the details next week," Shawn said. "I'll call you."

"All right." Rachel said happily. "I'll work out the details with Jenny and talk to you soon. Bye."

"Bye," he echoed. "And Rachel, thanks."

She hung up and turned to face Jenny's wide grin. "See, I told you. Nothing to it," Jenny said, laughing.

"Then why are my knees shaking?" Rachel gasped.

"Insulin reaction?" Jenny asked, a slight rise of alarm in her voice.

Rachel patted her friend's arm reassuringly. "Date fright. But I sense a quick recovery." She flashed a bright smile and started to her bedroom, her spirits soaring. She'd asked Shawn out and he'd said yes! "Come on, let's go pick out something for me to wear."

Twelve

ON the night of the dance, Rachel had butterflies as if she were going to perform a dance solo in front of a big audience. The arrangements were for Shawn's parents to bring him to her house and then join her parents for an evening of cards. Then Ben's dad was going to drive the four of them to the school. By the time she was actually in the car with Shawn, Ben, and Jenny, she felt ready to call the whole thing off. But the look on Shawn's face when he'd first seen her dressed in a new red print shirt and jeans, with her long hair freshly curled and her eyes sparkling with anticipation, made all the hassle worthwhile.

Once they were inside, Shawn took her hand and together they looked at how the school's library had been transformed by the dance committee. Live trees set in pots and adorned with tiny twinkle lights ringed the walls. Chairs were clustered around tables set along the back wall where kids gathered drinking punch and nibbling on popcorn. Colored spotlights bounced off couples dancing on the floor and a DJ from a local radio station sat on the stage spinning records. Even the faculty chaperones looked different from their everyday selves.

"Are you glad you came?" Rachel asked over the music.

"I have to admit, I was scared at first," he said, a half-teasing tone in his voice.

"Scared?" Rachel said, surprised. "Why?"

"Well, it's not every day I get to dance with a *real* dancer."

She giggled. "It's a different kind of dancing, silly."

"Show me."

Rachel let Shawn take her into his arms. They blended into the dancing couples, but somehow Rachel felt alone with Shawn.

"So are you ready for that big audition next month?" Shawn asked.

"Yes," Rachel answered truthfully. "I'm ready."

"I wish I could watch your tryouts."

"Sorry. No one's allowed to watch, not even parents. Madame Pershoff will take us to the studio where the auditions are being held, we'll fill out cards, get a number, and stand around being nervous until we're called to perform. Sometimes the judges take one look at you and dismiss you."

Shawn pulled back slightly. "What? Without you ever getting a chance to show your stuff? That's not fair."

She smiled at him. "That's the way it is. Ballerinas are supposed to have a certain look. If you don't, then they tell you good-bye."

He looked at her deeply. "Well, you look fine to me, Rachel Deering." Rachel rested her cheek on his chest. She closed her eyes and drifted on the soft waves of the music. "Who's your competition?" she heard him ask when the dance had ended and he was walking her toward the refreshment table.

Rachel searched the room until she found Melanie standing with Nick. "That girl over there is my main rival."

She watched Shawn study Melanie. Melanie looked good, as usual. She was dressed in shades of pink and her blond hair fell straight to her waist. She didn't want Shawn comparing her to Melanie. Melanie was prettier by far. "Is that her boyfriend with her?"

Rachel saw Nick standing next to Melanie. But his attention was focused on Donna Barkley, a pretty eighth grader. "Why, yes, it is."

"It looks like he's ignoring her."

Rachel blinked and studied them more closely. Nick was flirting openly with Donna. "He and Melanie have been together since school started. What a rude way for him to act." She couldn't keep the surprise out of her voice. Was Nick tired of Melanie and moving on to another girl? Rachel had heard stories about how Nick often led a girl on, then dropped her when he was sure she was his.

"Guys like that bug me," Shawn observed.

"Why?"

"It's like they think they're so cool treating people like dirt. No one has the right to be cruel to another person."

His anger surprised her. Why would Shawn care about something like that? Maybe a girl had treated him like Nick was treating Melanie. There was so much for her to learn about Shawn McLaughlin. Rachel felt a feeling of tenderness toward him. "Are we going to stand around all night talking about other people?" she asked softly. "Or are we going to dance?"

Shawn glanced at her and a slow, lazy smile spread across his face. The lights sent glints off his copper-colored hair. He traced a finger down the side of her jaw and she shivered. "We're going to dance," he said and took her in his arms. "This way I can tell all my friends that I once danced with a prima ballerina . . . before she became a star."

A melting sensation flowed through her and for the first time in her life she wondered what it would be like *not* to win the scholarship. She wondered what it would be like to spend the summer at home with Shawn McLaughlin.

* * * * *

The smell of orange blossoms was in the air as Rachel walked up the path to her house hand in hand with Shawn. Silver stars twinkled down from a black sky. The dance was over and Ben's dad had let them off, but she still felt as if she were swaying to the music of guitars and keyboards.

"I had fun. Thanks." Shawn told her.

"Me, too." They reached her front porch where her parents had left the light burning. "Do you think they heard the car?" Rachel asked.

"Are you kidding? My mother has 20/20 hearing."

"That's vision, silly."

"She has that, too."

Suddenly, Rachel was at a loss for something to say. She didn't want the night to end.

She felt cozy and comfortable with Shawn's arm draped over her shoulder.

"Don't go in yet," he said. "Have you got a tissue?"

"I think so . . ." She fumbled in her purse, curious at his strange request. "Why?" she asked as she handed him a wadded tissue.

Shawn reached into his pocket and brought out a dime and began to unscrew the rim of the porch light fixture. "What are you doing?"

"You'll see." He lifted the glass globe of the fixture off. Then he took the tissue and gingerly twisted the hot bulb until it blinked out. "I hate bright lights in my eyes," he whispered.

"My dad will be out in a flash," she whispered back.

"Maybe they have a hot hand of cards and won't notice."

"Maybe." Her blood rushed in her ears. She felt Shawn pull her toward him. "Why did you do that?" she asked.

"How can I kiss you goodnight with all that distracting light in my eyes?"

"I guess you couldn't . . ." Her voice trailed.

Shawn's forefinger lifted her chin slightly. Then he very softly and warmly brought his lips to hers.

* * * * *

The lobby of the North Miami Dance Studio was a whirlwind of activity. Over two hundred nervous dancers paced, lounged, or sat staring into space. Rachel entered the waiting area with Pat, Melanie, and Madame Pershoff.

"Where did all these dancers come from?" she asked.

"From as far away as Atlanta," Madame Pershoff said to Rachel. "The competition will be very stiff, but you three are my very best."

Rachel found a seat on the floor and filled out the card a staff member had handed her. She returned the card and was issued a number that Pat helped pin to her back. "Seventy-eight," she said. "Maybe it's my lucky number today."

The staff from the New York City's Ballet School of American Ballet, would call the girls into the main studio in groups of thirty. Rachel was relieved when Melanie and Pat were given much higher numbers. She didn't want the added tension of competing in the same group with Melanie. It was easier to go up against strangers.

Nervously she glanced at her watch and mentally calculated the hours between breakfast and her insulin injection. She'd better eat a granola bar before they called her inside. She looked for the bathroom, knowing that her case of nervous jitters would elevate her blood sugar and mean more trips there. Finally, she tucked her Medic Alert necklace into her bag. She didn't want the judges to know about her diabetes. At least not until the competition was over. She didn't want anything to count against her.

"Ladies! Please. Numbers 61 through 90. We are now ready for you," a small woman announced from the doorway of the studio.

"Here goes my future," Rachel mumbled under her breath. She took a deep breath and entered the vast studio where the master judges waited.

Thirteen

RACHEL recognized Mr. Tolavitch instantly. His distinctive head of white hair set him apart from the other judges. She wondered if he remembered meeting her at Madame Pershoff's Christmas concert. But when she gave him a pointed look, he didn't respond. She also recognized Anna Martova, one of the foremost dancers with the New York City Ballet. The woman was elegantly regal as she walked along the line of girls who were taking their places at the barre. As she passed them, she gathered their cards and surveyed them from head to toe.

Rachel stood still and straight, knowing that her body type was being evaluated. Some of the girls wouldn't pass this test. They wouldn't have the correct look, the right shape, or the right posture. Even an ounce of extra fat might make a difference. Rachel felt Ms. Martova's eyes looking her over. Rachel held her back straight and her arms gracefully loose at her sides. The great dancer jotted a note on Rachel's card and passed on down the line.

When she'd completed her scrutiny, Ms. Martova backed away. She crossed to the other judges and after speaking to them briefly, said, "Numbers 65, 72, 81, and 89—you may be excused."

The girls hurried out of the studio, most of them fighting back tears. Rachel felt sorry for them, but she was relieved that her number had not been called. At least she'd passed the first test.

A pianist began playing, and Ms. Martova issued instructions for various dance positions. "Fifth position. And *battement battu* . . . and *battement fondu* . . ." As Rachel moved through the steps, her confidence rose. She performed confidently, feeling energy pump through her body, giving her the power she needed to execute the moves.

She knew by heart what she would be judged on: muscle control, placement, turnout, poise, and passion. She concentrated on the music and her movements, not the judges, who were huddled together scribbling notes on cards. Again, Ms. Martova announced, "The following numbers may be dismissed . . ." She specified fifteen of the group and Rachel held her breath until she was positive she was one of the remaining eleven.

"Please move to the center of the floor," Ms. Martova instructed. "We will do half of the center work in soft shoe, then switch to pointe." Rachel knew that this was where her muscle control would count the most.

The work progressed until Ms. Martova said, "Thank you, ladies. You all have done well. In a few weeks, each of you will be notified by mail as to whether you have been awarded a full or partial scholarship, or are urged to try again next year. Your studio and instructor will also be contacted with the information. We appreciate your attendance for today's audition."

It's over, Rachel thought, as she collected her gear and went back to the lobby where the next group of girls waited to be called. She dropped to the floor in exhaustion but flashed Pat and Melanie a thumbs up sign and a smile. Pat returned her smile. Melanie did not. Rachel fished out another granola bar and ate it thoughtfully. In a way she felt sorry for Melanie. It must be boring to be so perfect.

She remembered Madame Pershoff telling her that she had the heart for the dance. She hoped that the judges had seen it today. In less than thirty minutes, a lifetime of effort had been judged. Had she impressed the judges? She'd given her best effort. A scholarship would either be offered to her or not. There was nothing left for her to do but wait.

* * * * *

That night at the dinner table, Rachel told her family all about the audition. Chris was the only one who showed any enthusiasm, clapping and squirming in her chair over each word. Her parents only gave polite remarks like, "That's nice, dear." It puzzled Rachel. She would have expected them to show more interest. Surely, they understood what getting to live in New York for six weeks and studying with the School of American Ballet meant to her!

But Jenny and Shawn's comments later in separate phone conversations made up somewhat for her parents' lack of interest.

When she described their indifference to Shawn, he told her, "Maybe they just don't want you to get your hopes up too much."

"Maybe . . . but they practically badgered me into resuming classes. Now they act like they don't care one way or the other."

"Nobody ever said parents weren't a strange species of adult," he answered.

Rachel giggled and went on to other things.

The days passed, but no letter arrived. School wound down to its final days. Dance classes settled into routine and Rachel's time with Shawn became more special, especially since he was so busy with soccer tournaments and competitions. When the phone rang late one evening, Rachel was surprised to hear Madame Pershoff's voice.

"I've just opened my mail, Rachel," she said.

Rachel's pulse quickened. "Yes, Ma'am."

"And the School of American Ballet has awarded five scholarships to dancers in the southeast—two full ones and three partials. And one of the full scholarships went to one of my girls!"

Rachel could scarcely breathe, the pressure was so strong. "Melanie?" she asked.

"Why, no, my dear. They have offered it to you."

For a few moments, Rachel couldn't say anything. Then she squealed and the words tumbled out nonstop. When her mother came to check out the noise, all Rachel could manage was, "I won! I won!"

After she'd hung up, she padded down the

hall behind her mother, babbling and dancing. In the kitchen, minutes later, she slowed down. Her mother's mouth was firmly set in a narrow frown. Rachel asked, "What's wrong, Mom? I thought you'd be glad that I've won."

Mrs. Deering turned and faced her daughter and Rachel could see that something was really wrong. Her mother wasn't excited for her one little bit. But Mrs. Deering said, "Congratulations, honey. Of course, I'm glad you've won."

"You aren't acting like it," Rachel insisted.

"I'm sorry. It's just so unexpected . . ."

"You didn't think I was good enough?" Rachel said with hurt in her voice.

"Just the opposite. I *always* knew you were good enough."

"Then what's the problem?"

Her mother dried her hands on a dish towel, twisting it around and around. "We have to talk, Rachel. Your father and I have discussed this and we were half-hoping it wouldn't come down to this." Rachel felt a sinking sensation in her stomach. Her mother continued, "You can't go, Rachel."

"What!" It was as if her mother had slapped her across the face with the dish towel. "What do you mean I can't go? Why can't I go? It's all I've been working for all these months . . ."

The tone in Rachel's voice was hysterical.

"Calm down. We have our reasons."

"Name them."

"New York is a big strange city . . ."

Rachel interrupted. "The school helps settle us in. They look out for the students. Madame Pershoff told me that students are closely watched and cared for."

"It's more than that."

Rachel studied her mother, catching the expression in her eyes. The answer hit Rachel unexpectedly. "It's my diabetes, isn't it?" she asked. "Yes, that's it. You're afraid of my diabetes. Afraid I won't take care of myself. You don't trust me."

"Stop it!" Mrs. Deering commanded. "Of course, we trust you. You've been an excellent patient once you began accepting your disease. It has nothing to do with your lack of responsibility."

"Then why? *Why?*" Rachel felt tears in her eyes.

Mrs. Deering reached out to her, but Rachel yanked away. "Try to see it from our point of view," Mrs. Deering reasoned. "You'll be over fifteen hundred miles from home. Away from us, your doctors, your support. What about your meals and your special diet? Who'll fix them? And what if you get sick and your blood sugar goes out of control? Or what if you have a severe reaction? You know how serious the consequences of untreated insulin reactions are."

"I know," Rachel said. "But I'm so careful. I won't be pushed around by fears of insulin reactions." Her statement sounded grown-up even to her own ears.

"And I don't want you to be. Perhaps when you're older . . ."

"But they're offering the scholarship now," Rachel pleaded. "I can't turn it down. You've always encouraged my dancing. I can't stop now."

"Your dancing is wonderful." Her mother leaned forward for emphasis. "And it's wonderful for your diabetic control—"

"But what about *me*? Don't you understand? I want to dance for me, not for my diabetic control. All my life I've dreamed of this. I've dreamed of being a professional dancer and now I have the chance and you won't let me because of my stupid old diabetes. I *have* to take that scholarship, Mom." Now Rachel couldn't stop the flow of tears.

Her mother grew rigid. "I'm sorry, Rachel. We can't take the chance. We can't let you go. Perhaps your father can explain it better than I."

"You can't do this to me! You can't." Rachel was unable to speak further. Sobs were choking her throat. Rachel ran from the kitchen and shut herself away in her bedroom. She cried until her eyes were red and swollen. But her mother never came to say she'd changed her mind, that it was all a mistake and certainly she could go.

When she was able to control her voice, she dialed Shawn from the hall phone. He wasn't home. Where could she go for help? Who could she turn to? Then she remembered what Dr. Malar had said. "If you ever have any problems, Rachel, call me." Well, she had problems now.

Shakily, she again picked up the receiver. What would she say? She'd never called a doctor before. Her parents had always done those things. She found the doctor's number and dialed it, determined to talk to him.

His answering service picked up. "May I help you?"

"I need to talk to Dr. Malar. This is Rachel Deering."

"Is this an emergency?"

"No. I–I mean, yes. I'm one of his patients and I just have to talk to him. Please . . ." Her voice cracked.

"I'll have him paged," the woman's voice

assured Rachel. "What is your telephone number?"

Rachel gave the number, hung up, and waited by the phone. She knew she'd have to grab it on the first ring, before her mother could answer it from the kitchen. She sat in the darkened hall, clenching and unclenching her fists in nervousness.

The phone jangled, and Rachel jerked up the receiver. "Hello," she whispered.

"Rachel? This is Dr. Malar."

Fresh tears swam into her eyes. "Oh, Dr. Malar. Help me. Please . . . help me!"

Fourteen

RACHEL couldn't sit still. She jiggled her leg, impatient for her parents to complete their discussion with Dr. Malar. Her eyes darted around his office. Dr. Malar sat behind a large oak desk littered with papers, file folders, and stacks of pink phone messages.

"So you see," Mr. Deering was saying, "while we're proud of Rachel's achievement, we can't send her off alone to New York for half of the summer. We feel there's too much risk involved."

Dr. Malar's blue eyes were thoughtful. Rachel remembered how she'd sobbed out her problem to him over the phone the night before. He had been very kind to her. He'd said, "Tell them I want to see all of you in my office tomorrow. Call in the morning to arrange a time with my receptionist. And Rachel . . ." his tone was soft and soothing,

". . . get a good night's sleep and don't dwell on this. We'll see what can be worked out."

Now, judging from her parents' looks, it didn't seem possible that Dr. Malar could help her at all. Dr. Malar said, "I appreciate your concerns, Mr. Deering, but New York is not exactly the backwoods of America, you know. I'm well-acquainted with several qualified pediatric endocrinologists there and feel confident that I can call and have her case covered by any one of them temporarily."

Rachel felt new hope. Her mother interjected, "It's not only medical reasons—"

"I understand," Dr. Malar told her. "But if Rachel were not a diabetic, would you have the same concerns?" Neither of her parents answered. "Look, Rachel's come a long way since her diagnosis and her initial and typical behavior reactions. First, disbelief, then anger, rejection and finally, acceptance." He numbered the stages on his hand for emphasis.

Rachel had learned the stages in her support group. She remembered how hostile and demanding she'd been in the beginning.

Dr. Malar continued. "The important thing is that she *did* come to grips with it. She did resume her dancing. She did join the support group." *Because of Shawn*, Rachel reminded herself silently. *If it hadn't been for Shawn . . .*

"She continues to take excellent care of herself. Her blood sugar monitoring shows her to be in acceptable ranges, her lab work proves that her blood chemistry is well within normal parameters . . . in short, medically speaking, there's no reason to keep her home."

"But–but there's so much responsibility involved," Mrs. Deering said, a pleading tone in her voice.

"That's true. And there always will be. She has to take care of herself for the rest of her life. And the quality of that care will determine the quality of her life. Don't base your decision on her disease. Make your decision on what's best for Rachel. She's bright and mature, and most important, she's not afraid." Dr. Malar looked at Rachel and she looked hard back at him. "Not being afraid is the most important factor of all. Think very carefully before you tell her no."

Rachel felt thankful for Dr. Malar's comments. She looked at her parents' faces and saw an expression that gave her hope. Dr. Malar's words had made an impression. She hoped it was enough of an impression for them to change their minds and let her go. Didn't they realize that they were deciding her whole future?

* * * * *

That night, Shawn's mother came to Rachel's house. Shawn had asked her to come to help plead Rachel's case. "We went through the same thing when my soccer team started to travel out-of-state for tournaments," Shawn had told Rachel over the phone. "My mom's an expert on diabetes and traveling."

In the Deering living room, Rachel listened to the conversation between her parents and Mrs. McLaughlin. It was her life they were hashing over, but she had no input. Although it was hard to keep silent and listen, she managed, mostly because Shawn had told her that his mother ". . . could persuade an Eskimo to buy an air conditioner."

"I'll never forget the first time Shawn's soccer team went away on an overnighter," Mrs. McLaughlin began once the Deerings had finished listing their reasons and concerns. "Shawn was ten years old and the team had a big championship match to play in Orlando. They were to go up the day before, spend the night, and be at the field by nine in the morning. Well, I just couldn't stand the thought of him managing without me." A smile flipped the corners of her mouth. "So I went along. There were sixteen little soccer players, three coaches . . . and me. I know that Shawn was embarrassed to death."

Rachel's mother interrupted, "Yes, but that was for one night. This trip is for six *weeks*." Rachel groaned inwardly.

Mrs. McLaughlin continued. "The next time, they went to play a tournament in Washington, D.C. Naturally, I knew he couldn't make it without me, so I packed up and joined him again." Rachel realized that Shawn's mother was poking fun at herself for her over-protectiveness. Then her tone turned serious. "But I'm glad I went because this trip gave me a confidence about him that I'd never gotten otherwise. He did fine. Yes, he had some problems—a reaction because the team ran behind schedule sightseeing in the Smithsonian Institute and didn't get lunch on time—but he coped. He took care of himself."

She paused and Rachel turned her attention to her parents. They were deeply engrossed in Mrs. McLaughlin's comments. "I stopped trailing along to every tournament two years ago—unless of course, I go to see him play. I came to understand that Shawn was a soccer player who had diabetes, not a diabetic soccer player. The difference may seem small, but it *is* important."

For a moment, there was a heavy silence in the room. Rachel could hear the grandfather clock ticking in the hallway as she watched the thoughtful expressions of her parents. Slowly, she began to feel hopeful.

"I don't know . . ." Mrs. Deering said, confusion sounding in her voice.

"Go with her," Mrs. McLaughlin urged.

"What?"

"Go with her. Get her settled in, contact her doctors, and stay a few days until you're sure she's all right. Then come home. That way, you won't feel like you're sending her off into the unknown. And I'll bet Rachel will feel better about it, too. Won't you, Rachel?"

Mrs. McLaughlin turned to Rachel. Slowly, Rachel nodded. It was true. She would feel better about it. As anxious as she was to go, she was also scared. If her mother helped square things away with the school and contacted the doctors, she would be relieved. That way, she would be able to really concentrate on her dancing. "Please, Mom?" Rachel added. "We can do it together."

Mrs. McLaughlin rose. "I hope you change your minds, because this is more than just a dance scholarship. For Rachel, it's a pattern for the rest of her life. Either she controls her diabetes, or it controls her."

* * * * *

123

"Look at me!" Chris called from in front of the airline ticket counter at Miami International Airport. She'd looped two luggage tags over her ears and they dangled like gigantic earrings. Rachel giggled at her sister.

"Have you got your seat assignments?" her father asked his wife.

"Yes, and are you sure you can get Chris to dance classes and the orthodontist while I'm away?"

"Good grief," Mr. Deering said. "You're only going for a week. Chris and I can manage."

Rachel fidgeted with the waistband of her slacks. She was more excited and nervous than she'd ever expected to be about the plane trip to New York. She searched the crowds in the ticket area for Shawn. She knew that she and her mother would soon have to board the plane. Would he be able to make it to see her off?

Chris tugged on her arm. "Are you going to buy me something in New York?"

Her bright smiling eyes made a small lump rise in Rachel's throat. Six whole weeks away from home. At first, the thought had thrilled her. Now, telling Chris good-bye for such a long time made her feel sentimental. "Sure, I'll buy you something. And will you take good care of my record collection?"

Chris' eyes grew round. "Can I? You don't mind if I keep it in my room?"

"Just be careful with it," Rachel warned, softening her comment with a smile.

Then Rachel felt an arm slip around her middle and spin her about.

"Hi." She stared into Shawn's blue eyes. "Sorry I'm late, but my friend Joel drove me and we had to park on the upper decks."

Rachel felt moved that he'd come at all. "No problem. They're not boarding our plane yet."

"Are you all set?"

Rachel concentrated on Shawn and hardly noticed the crowds swarming around them. "I hope so."

"Send me a postcard."

"I'll send you one a week." Now she was going, really going. Suddenly she realized how much she would miss Shawn. Would he forget her in six weeks? Would he find another girlfriend who would be available all summer? She thought of the girls in the support group and how much some of them flirted with Shawn. "Will you miss me?"

A grin shone on his face. "Only if you want me to."

A slow blush crept up her cheeks. "Miss me. And that's an order."

He laughed. "Here, take this to remember

me by." He slipped a roll of candy into her hand.

She squeezed it tightly in her palm, feeling the warmth left over from his touch.

"Rachel, we've got to go to our gate." Rachel heard her mother's voice say.

She followed her mother and at the "Passengers Only" sign hugged her dad and sister good-bye. She wanted to hug Shawn, too, but couldn't in front of her family.

"Knock 'em dead," Shawn called as she and her mother headed up the long carpeted stretch toward their waiting plane.

"I will," she promised, then turned and waved good-bye.

For the first time in a long time, Rachel felt really happy. After New York, after training and dancing with top ballet masters, she had Shawn to come home to. Life had a way of working out. Dreams had a way of coming true. Dreams she could chase for the rest of her life.

If you would like more information about diabetes, please contact:

The Juvenile Diabetes Research Foundation
8600 N.W. 53rd Terrace
Miami, Florida 33166

About the Author

LURLENE MCDANIEL made up her first story in second grade, wrote a play in fourth grade, and wrote a book in high school. She graduated from college and became a copywriter, writing ad campaigns for hundreds of clients. Now, when Lurlene is not writing books, she writes a column for a Christian magazine, and teaches writing.

Young readers from all over the country write to Lurlene to say how much they enjoy her books. They often ask the question, "Where do you get your ideas?" Lurlene says that ideas are everywhere, on television news programs, in newspapers, and even in her own children. She uses her family and friends as character samples. Her background includes modeling, television, and a fondness for horses.

Writing books about kids overcoming sensitive problems like cancer, diabetes, and divorce draw a wide response from her readers.

Lurlene lives in Tallahassee, Florida with her two sons, who are both active soccer players.

Other books by Lurlene McDaniel include *Six Months to Live, If I Should Die Before I Wake,* and *Sometimes Love Just Isn't Enough.*